Revelations

Yolanda M. Johnson

Literary Wonders! Media Group

Literary Wonders!
Media Group
Greensboro

This book is a work of fiction. Names, characters, places and incidents are products of the author's imagination or are used fictitiously. However, some instances and events are true and names have been changed to protect the innocent *and* the guilty.

ISBN 10:   0-977-0433-X
ISBN 13:   978-0-977-04033-9
Library of Congress Control Number: 2012901456

Cover design by **Dana Pittman and Pittman Unlimited**
Printed in the United States of America

Also by
Yolanda M. Johnson

My Daughter's Keeper
Circumstances

Anthologies
Crimes of Passion: The Anthology
She Has a Big 'But'!: Get Past Your Excuses & Realize Your
Dreams

In Loving Memory of

Oscar Mayfield Hill Jr.

June 17, 1950 – October 29, 2008

Praises for *Circumstances* by Yolanda M. Johnson-Bryant

"*Circumstances* is an engaging tale of a daughter's quest to find inner peace while dealing with a dysfunctional relationship with her mother. Yolanda M. Johnson touches on issues that may shock you; however you won't be able to pull yourself away from the pages." --*Shelia M. Goss , Essence Magazine's Best Selling Author of My Invisible Husband and Dallas Morning News Best Selling Author of Roses Are Thorns, Violets are True*

"*Circumstances* draws the reader in from the intriguing introduction. It is a passionate story that teleports the reader into the minds and lives of the characters. The dialog is conversational and as you read you hear the perspectives of the characters, their conflict, and their anguish. I believe author Yolanda Johnson has written an empathetically real and unique story that is as easy to love as it is to read."--*Bennie Patridge III "The MANual*

"Yolanda Johnson is a powerful new voice in the literary world. *Circumstances* leaves you wanting more!" --*Sylvia Willis Lett - I Wish I Had Waited" Dallas Morning News #1 Best seller*

"From the opening page to the dramatic ending, **CIRCUMSTANCES** is a powerful tale of love and forgiveness. Johnson pulls no punches as she vividly describes the mental, emotional and physical impact of abuse and not just to the victim." –*Monique Bruner Delta Reviewer" Real Page Turners*

A Note from the Author

I'm often asked, *Yolanda, what genre do you write?* And, my answer is always, *I don't like to categorize my writing. I don't like being put in a box. If I absolutely had to generalize my writing, I would say that I mostly write about women's issues. I've written and will continue to write about issues that women face in my fiction and non-fiction works, whether they be health issues, relationship issues, mental issues, personal or professional issues.*

As stated above, I say mostly because I am currently working on a children, tween *and* teen series, a book about diabetes and a mystery thriller series. In addition, I am working on a few professional and self-help titles. So, I say to you, don't put me in a box. I am bursting at the seams and you'll never know which side I'll emerge from next.

It is my wish that *whatever* I choose or am inspired to write, that you will enjoy my work, and most of all that you will get something out of what I write. I want my writing to change lives.

I pray that you enjoy **Revelations**. It is strongly encouraged that you read *Circumstances*, as **Revelations** is the sequel to that novel. Although, **Revelations** can stand on its own, reading *Circumstances* will help readers better understand the life that is Renee Matthews.

God Bless!

Yolanda M. Johnson

Acknowledgements

I must always thank God for all that I do. For without his gifts and blessings, I am null and void.

Thank you, to my husband, Gregory Bryant for being an understanding and supportive husband, allowing me to follow my dreams . . . and pay for most of it. Thank you for distressing the stressful days, helping with deadlines, taking on cooking, housework and other chores, while I burned the midnight oil and continually follow my dream. You are the best. I love you so much.

Thank you to those women in my life, both real and fictional, who give me material to work with and inspiration to tell stories.

A special thanks to Tee C. Royal and RAWSISTAZ Literary Agency for your support. Much love to my RAWSISTAZ, and my special sisters, Kim Floyd, Tina Brooks McKinney, Candace Cottrell, Gayle Sloan Jackson, Mary Crawford, Monique Bruner, Tawanna Price, Toni Robinson and Chanel Renee. If I forgot anyone, please charge my head, not my heart.

Special thanks to my literary sisters, Shelia Goss, Victoria Christopher Murray, Dana Pittman, Bonnie Calhoun and Jean Bailey Robor. Again, if I've missed anyone, please charge my head, or my senility, and not my heart.

Shout outs to Patricia Hall, my Toastmasters family, John Wooden, Kristen Eckstein, Sue Falcone, Angel Guerrero III (You are the best mentor a lady could ask for), Cathy Daniels Lee, Janet Harllee, Jeff Rivera, Regina Taylor (love you sis, you've always been so supportive of me), Pam Perry, Renee Estrada, Yalonda Benford, Rosa Ferguson, Sonja Wright, Tyora Moody, Julie Jurado (Love you Mummy), to my prince

Ty, keep your head up, I have every faith in you, Duena Watkins and Shannon Nicole.

Thank you to my sister-in-law, Tamarra Bryant for helping me with reading and editing projects.

In special memory of Leslie Esdaile Banks (aka L.A. Banks), such a beautiful soul. May you rest in peace.

If I have forgotten anyone, as always, please forgive me. It was not on purpose.

The Beautiful Place

Lyrics by Tonex
(Pronounced Toe-Nay)

Since I was born I heard about this place
Where there is always sunshine and everyday is a Sunday
There will be no more rain no more skies that are gray
Oh, they tell me of an uncloudy day

All my life I've heard about this beautiful place
It's somewhere beyond the galaxy and outer space
Where the streets are gold as glass and sheer with transparency
Where we shout and sing His praise throughout eternity

As I grew old, I wondered 'bout this place
Will I ever get there; how much longer will I have to wait?
Then I felt a sensation from my head down to my face
On a Tuesday afternoon I felt my body change
I've been raptured!

All my life I dreamed about this beautiful place
And I can't believe my eyes I really see His face
Reunited with my loved ones walking hand in hand
And the Holy River intertwines with emerald sand

"Oh, my God, the flowers sing!!!"
As pure white horses kneel down
For the King has made His entrance at the trumpets' sound
As we sing His throne changes from blue to aqua-marine
And to shades of indigo unlike you've ever seen

No more death, no more pain
Joy, everlasting Zion sings Holy, Holy, Holy
Oh, Hallelujah, Hallelujah, Hallelujah
We have over come

English: We have over come
Japanese: Maki-na ka-ata (we have defeated our enemy)
Spanish: Cantemos, bailemos (let us sing, let us dance)
Swahili: Harambee (let us come together)

Chapter 1

November 3, 1968

Rosie continued rocking in her shabby rocking chair as she watched Jessie Lee walk Dr. Reynolds down the rickety porch—down the cracked, dirty, make-shift walkway, and out to the dirt road that the good doctor had just ventured.

Dr. Reynolds hadn't told them anything that she didn't already know. It wasn't like this was the first time that Jessie Lee had gone too far, and it wasn't the first time a baby was conceived.

Rosie thought about the current inconvenience that Jessie Lee and Barbara Jean had brought on the family. She had always dismissed past acts by reasoning to herself that Barbara Jean wasn't one of *them* anyhow. After all, the other children had Jessie Lee's last name—Barbara Jean did not. She was an outsider to most, not one of *them*.

Jessie Lee had decided that Rosie would lie to the powers that be and say that she was a single mother and her unborn child's father had abandoned them. She was told that this was the only way she could get help at the county hospital. She needed medical help—*and* she was colored.

She went along with Jessie Lee's plan for the longest time. The townspeople not only knew that Barbara Jean was born out of wedlock, but they also thought it was mighty kind that Jessie Lee would raise a child that wasn't his own. They could never find out that Barbara Jean was, in fact, Jessie Lee's flesh and blood. They could never find out that Barbara Jean was the result of Jessie Lee forcing himself upon Rosie in a drunken stupor.

"So what we gone do?" Rosie asked Jessie Lee when his six-foot-four shell walked back through the wobbly screen door.

"We gone get rid'a it," he answered.

"Whatchu' mean, get rid'a it?"

"She can't have that baby hea'. Matta fact, we need to get rid of *huh*. She gone tell somebody and thas gone brang disgrace to dis' fam'ly."

"Mighty funny you thank about that now, since you swoe you wudn't gone do it no moe."

"What is you talkin' crazy fah' woman?"

"Don't play wit' me Jessie Lee. You don't thank I be knowin' what be goin' on when me and da kids leave dis' hea house?"

Jessie Lee didn't want to hear any part of what Rosie had to say, but he didn't have any choice. In his attempt to escape to the kitchen that was so small, the food box sat outside the back door, Jessie knew Rosie was hot on his heels.

"The las' time she got hurt, Jessie Lee, you said you wasn't gone touch huh no moe."

"I ain't touch huh!" Jessie Lee yelled at Rosie.

"I know you don't want me ta go in dea' and ask huh do you?" Rosie stood her ground—her hands on her hips, she leaned her four-foot-ten-inch frame against the doorway—her housecoat worn and faded.

"You ain't gone ask nobody nuttin'. I said I ain't touch huh. We just gotta find a way to fix dis' mess."

Rose said a silent prayer to God that, like all the other times, He would get them out of their current mess. She couldn't understand why Jessie Lee thought she was stupid and she never could understand why Jessie Lee couldn't keep his hands to himself. God knows she tried pleasing him, but between taking care of all the children, cleaning white folk's houses and cooking and cleaning, she could only give him what she could give him. But she reckoned even if she could give herself completely to her husband, his hands would still find a reason to wander.

Although he had a roving eye, Jessie Lee had never been the kind to cheat on Rosie, with someone in the street—at least not that *she* knew of. No sir, he chose to do his dirt behind closed doors . . . *their* closed doors. Yes, he laid his hat . . . at home. And what he did at home, well now, that wasn't cheating—because she allowed it.

"So what we gone do dis' time huh?" Rosie demanded. "You can't keep huh locked up in hea' fo'eva. She gone tell *somebody*."

"She ain't gone tell nobody, 'cause we gone send huh away."

"Send huh where?"

"Ta'morrah, you needs ta go to the market and call yo' sista."

"Who?" Rosie inquired.

"Wanda," Jessie Lee said with authority. Wanda was Rosie's baby sister and she had moved from the south long ago. She had said she wanted to be free and decided to moved out west to Colorado. Wanda had found herself a decent solider, got married, settled down, and had children. Even though Rosie didn't want to have to explain the embarrassing details to Wanda, she knew that Colorado would be the best place for Barbara Jean—and their *little* secret.

"So you want me ta call *my* sista and ask huh iffen' she can take care of our baby girl and huh unbone' baby?"

"Naw. I want huh to take in Barbara Jean, but she can't have dat baby. No way, no how. She gots to get ridd'a it."

Rosie looked at Jessie Lee in disbelief. None of this would be happening if Jessie Lee had kept his carnal desire confined to his own marital bed. Rosie hated Jessie Lee for what he had done to her little girl, but she was a poor black woman in Louisiana. Where was she going to go with five children? She had no other choice and Jessie Lee provided the best he could for his family.

Wanda had told Rosie that she was always welcomed to come out west and stay with her whenever she decided to leave Jessie Lee, but that was four children ago. And she hadn't even told Jessie Lee that she was pregnant—again. She knew it. She had all the signs—she had had them for weeks now. Even though Jessie Lee found her own daughter more desirable than her, he felt it was his right to have her, whenever he wanted—whether she wanted him or not.

November 4, 1968

Rosie woke the next morning with the rising sun. She wanted to get the children fed, dressed and off to school.

"Mama, is I goin' ta school ta'day?" Barbra Jean asked standing in the doorway of the kitchen. She was dressed in a long black skirt and one of Jessie Lee's old work shirts, her hair in two crooked pigtails.

Rosie couldn't bear to look at Barbra Jean. She was this child's mother and she was supposed to love and protect her. She hadn't done either. Deep down inside, Rosie resented Barbara Jean. Jessie Lee was only supposed want *her* and Barbara Jean got in the middle of that, but at the same time, she knew, it was her own fault. She prayed that somewhere in Barbara Jean's future, she could learn to forgive her—forgive her for feeding her to the wolves.

Rosie poured more cornmeal into the hot skillet that sat on top of the hot burner. "Naw, baby. Not ta'day," was all she said. Rosie didn't see the tear that escaped Barbara Jean's eye as she headed out the back door to do her routine, daily chores.

After the other children were off to school, Rosie stood in the frame of the back door and called out to Barbara Jean.

"Bob'ra Jean," she called to her.

"Ma'am?" Barbara Jean responded.

"C'mon and go wit' me to the market." Rosie knew she could not take back all that Jessie Lee had done, but she would be damned if she left Barbara Jean alone with Jessie Lee another moment.

Barbara Jean followed her mother down the dirt road in silence as she kicked rocks, a game she always played when she traveled the dirt road. Rosie watched as her daughter got lost in child's play. It was as if it were the first time she had seen her daughter's innocence. But that had been before, Barbara Jean was with child. It was Jessie Lee's intention to abort the baby, but Rosie would make sure that Wanda knew that aborting the baby, was not an option.

After Rosie hung up the phone, everything was all set. Barbara Jean would be on a train headed to Colorado in just a few short hours. She took Wanda's advice that Barbara Jean should not spend another night in the Jackson house and she was furious at Rosie for allowing this to happen.

When Wanda asked Rosie if Jessie Lee had done anything to any of the other children, specifically Rosie's other daughter, Rosie told her no. Wanda didn't believe her, but it was going to be a stretch taking care of a teenage mother and her child, let alone additional mouths to feed.

Chapter 2

It took a moment for me to adjust my eyes, but eventually everything became clear. Charlie, my best friend, was standing over me and I suddenly realized that I was lying on the ground. I could hear loud chatter coming from every direction as people talked amongst themselves. I heard selective *oohs, ahhs* and *dear lords*.

I tried to make sense of what had just transpired. I was walking through the garden and down the makeshift sandy aisle towards the beach to meet Stuart. I was to become Mrs. Stuart Humphries, but the devil had reared *her* ugly head.

My mother had interrupted my wedding with the bombshell of the century. I took a moment to catch my breath as the words she had just said replayed in my head. If it weren't for the reaction of the crowd, I would have thought that perhaps I was losing my mind. But I wasn't. Could Stuart really be my father? Did he and my mother really have an intimate relationship? The thought of it all made me nauseous.

"Renee, are you okay?" Charlie asked me as I looked around. No, I wasn't, and judging by Charlie's red clammy skin, neither was he. I looked to my right and there my mother stood, glaring at Stuart and sucking her teeth. She was wearing a green hounds tooth ensemble with four-inch snake-skin pumps, falsifying her four-foot-eleven frame. It was eighty-five degrees in Coronado—who does that? Her Fashion Fair make-up was beading and sweat was rolling down the sides of face.

The hatred in Stuart's eyes spoke volumes. He was being detained by three of his groomsmen. It was obvious he wanted to choke the life out of Barbara Jean but she stood her ground as if she dared him to do anything.

"How could you be so evil and so bitter?" he asked her. I watched the exchange between the two. Charlie held me as if he was never going to let me go.

"I tole you, if you eva cross me, you was gone be sorry," my mother hissed.

"I have no clue what you're talking about." Stuart held his hands up as in defeat. "You pick now? Your daughter's wedding? Your *own* daughter? Are you kidding me?" Stuart had a million questions and he was asking them as they came to him. I had a million questions too, but he seemed to be doing a good job at asking.

"You had to have known before now. Why am *I* just finding out? Why are *we* just now finding out?" Stuart asked her. *Good question* I thought to myself.

"What was I 'sposed ta say after that tramp ansa'd yo' door and told me it was ova 'tween us?" Barbara Jean spat. Stuart looked dumbfounded as if he was trying to remember.

"What in the hell are you talking about BJ?"

BJ I thought.

He even had a pet name for her. I watched as my future slowly started to dissipate.

"The day when you was leavin' for college and I came to yo' house and . . ." she started, but Stuart interrupted her. Judging by his expression, he remembered the very moment Barbara Jean was referring to.

"It *was* the day I left for college. When I came to the door, you had left. You were so far down the road. I called for you but you kept going, and at that point, I felt there was no use in stopping you," he said. He sat on a nearby chair. "You had on a halter top and shorts," he reminisced. "I called out to you, but you didn't hear me. It was my cousin. It was my cousin that answered the damn door!"

"Umhmm, I bet she was yo' cousin, and Bill Clinton is my brotha." My mother took a few steps forward and continued talking. "She tole me you had dis' great life planned and I wasn't gone be no part of it."

Stuart held his head in hands trying to control his sadness *and* his anger, but his tears had a mind of their own.

"That was over thirty years ago BJ. Are you telling me that you've been holding a grudge for *thirty* years? Do you mean to tell me that after all this time, you would go through this much trouble to ruin your own daughter's wedding just to pay *me* back?

"What the hell was I sposed' to do or say?"

"How about, hey asshole, by the way, I'm pregnant! Or . . . or how about, hey Renee, thirty years ago I was intimate with the man you are about to marry and there's a big possibility that he may be your father! Oh wait . . . here's one, how about, hey Stuart you can't marry Renee because she is *our* daughter?" Stuart shouted.

"Payback is a mutha fucka ain't it?" she asked. That took me off guard. It was almost as if she had slapped me across the face. My mother snickered and turned to leave the makeshift garden on the same path that I had journeyed just moments prior. I wanted to run behind her, put her in a choke hold and squeeze her until the last breath of air left her body, but my feet felt like they were stuck in quick sand and a pool of unbelief—the audacity of this woman.

"But your *own* daughter?" Stuart called out behind her.

My mother stopped in her tracks and turned around. "That bitch had what was comin' ta huh' too." My mother spit on the ground in my direction as if I was a dirty dog off the street, and then she turned and disappeared into the main villa of the hotel.

"This isn't over," Stuart shouted to her. "You better believe this is not over. Not by a long shot." I grabbed his arm. My mother wasn't worth him going to jail. She was well past bitter—well past hurt—well past hope. Why else would she be so evil? What had happened to her? Who had hurt her so badly? I couldn't imagine that person being Stuart. Not the kind man that I had opened up my heart to, so much so that I was willing to call him *husband.*

Stuart jumped and pulled his arm back when he realized it was me. At that moment, we both felt our worlds disconnect and we knew that there would be no wedding, not now, not ever. Even if he *wasn't* my father, there was no way we could be together. There was no way the two of us could ever be husband and wife.

Charlie's pale skin was beet red by now as he gave Stuart a knowing glance in which Stuart nodded in acknowledgement.

"She succeeded in what she came to do," he told Charlie.

I had almost forgotten the beach garden was full of guests. I stood up to meet the crowd. I wanted to give words of apology but embarrassment engulfed me and I felt weak and nearly lost my balance.

"You got her?" Charlie asked Stuart.

"Yes," Stuart answered, holding me up. Charlie took hold of the microphone.

"Ladies and gentlemen, on behalf of Stuart and Renee, I would like to apologize for . . . for this fiasco and for *any* inconvenience that it may have caused any of you. At times, things are beyond our control and we have to make the best of them. I know I speak for Renee and Stuart when I say, just by your being here, they know that they are loved. With that being said, there is plenty of food in the reception hall. I believe Gerald and Tonex will continue to provide our entertainment for the afternoon and I would hate to see it all go to waste."

I began to feel weaker by the second. There had to be over a few hundred people that had come out to see Stuart and I exchange vows. Now, over a few hundred people had the leading scoop on my fiasco of a wedding.

"So please feel free to stay and mingle, eat, dance and be merry." Charlie finished, and placed the microphone back on its stand.

"Let's get her out of here," he told Stuart, as we headed back into the main villa.

When we got into the foyer, Marlene, my former best friend, was talking on the house phone. She was wearing a white dress that left very little to the imagination. Her auburn weave cascaded down her bare back. I walked over to her, snatched the antique phone from her hand, and put it on its cradle. I was ready to throw down.

"Why are you still here?" I asked her sternly. The more I looked at her, the more anger welled up inside me.

"Don't get mad at me!" she snapped. She had one hand on her hip, pointed her finger at me as she bobbled her head and rotated her neck. I reached for her throat but Stuart grabbed me.

"Get out!" he and Charlie shouted unanimously. Somehow, I knew that if Marlene was still here, Barbara Jean was somewhere lurking, waiting to strike again.

"We need to make sense of this mess Stu, but in the meantime, Renee will be staying with me in San Francisco," I heard Charlie say.

"I agree, she shouldn't be alone right now." He turned to me, "But, Renee when you are up to it, I want to take a DNA test to confirm all of this. I wouldn't put anything past Barbara Jean. None of this makes any sense." Stuart paced back and forth trying to come up with some sort of explanation to our unfolding drama.

He gazed towards the French doors that led outside to the front of the villa. "I do remember right before I left for college. Rumor had it that her father had raped her," he said above a whisper and to no one in particular. I looked at him like he had lost his mind.

"My Paw wouldn't do anything like that!" I charged at him. How dare he speak that way of my late grandfather.

"Renee I really don't know *what* happened. I just don't believe for a moment that I'm your father," Stuart defended himself.

"I want to do it before we go to Frisco," I said. Stuart had attacked a personal side of me and at that particular moment, I needed a way to denounce him.

"Do what?" Charlie asked. Stuart seemed just as confused.

"Blood tests."

"Are you sure Luv?" Charlie asked me.

"Yes, I want to get this over with as soon as possible. I just can't go without knowing."

"We'll go Monday," Stuart agreed. I clung to Charlie's chest. I couldn't bear to touch Stuart.

† † †

I sat on a bench that was located under the bay window in my mini-villa and gazed down at the scenery. Losing myself for a moment, I took in the beautiful foliage—the flowers in bloom and plush palm trees. The faint sight of the ocean's mist took me to a paradise of peace. What I wouldn't give to be in a place without a care or a hurt in the world . . . *the beautiful place.*

I was in love with Stuart. He was in love with me. We were soul mates and now we had to let go of that love. We both knew that no matter what the results of that test would be, both of us would be mending broken hearts.

A sharp pain in my side interrupted my brief getaway. Gas maybe? Perhaps nervousness. After the slight distraction, I attempted to find the beautiful place once more but was unsuccessful. I took in the rest of the scenery. To my right I could see other mini villas, white sandy beaches and aqua blue waters for miles. Paradise could be seen from this very window.

What were the chances of this happening? And to me of all people. I had a gut feeling that something would happen at my wedding. But nothing like this. If I had a child, I would never do anything to hurt them, let alone do something so devastating. But then again, I don't know why I was so shocked, after all, Barbara Jean *was* Barbara Jean.

I found myself, *slowly*, drifting back to that place that I tried so desperately not to. I went back to a time when I was eight years old. Barbara Jean and her boyfriend Hal had gotten into yet another argument. Even at the innocent age of eight, Barbara Jean saw me as a threat.

"Renee, brang yo' ass in hea' right now!" she screamed.

"Yes ma'am," I said making a prompt exit from dreamland. I jumped out of bed and rushed to her bedroom.

"Yes Ma'am?" I said again once I reached her doorway.

"What I done tole you 'bout bein' in dis house when Hal hea?" I was dumbfounded by her question, because I was still half sleep and really didn't recall her telling me anything. I shrugged my shoulders, gesturing my cluelessness. Before I knew it, my mother had slapped me on the side of my face—so hard that the stinging pain felt somewhat like brain freeze.

"I'm gone ask you one mo' time. What I tell you 'bout being in dis' house when Hal hea'?"

"Um," was all I could get out. This time she hit me with her fist. I saw white spots and then blackness as I fell to the floor.

"You better not hit that girl again," I heard Hal say. "That's all you do to those damn kids is abuse them and talk down to them. All the girl did was fix me some eggs. Damn!"

"I done tole her fass ass if you in tha house, she betta leave."

"And where is she supposed to go?"

"I don't give a damn. She jes' bet not be in dis' house witch you when nobody ain't hea'."

"What? You think I'm going to do something to her? Hell, she's like a daughter to me," Hal said in amazement. "I've treated both those kids like they were my own and you think that I'm going to mess with them? Why am I even here?" he asked.

"It ain't you I'm worried 'bout," Barbara Jean told him. "She's the one I don't trust," Barbara Jean said.

"What the hell are you talking about with your crazy ass? The girl is only eight."

"That don't mean shit. I know how fass these girls is."

Hal looked at my mother and threw his hands up in unbelief. "Un-fucking-believable. You've got to be kidding me," he said right before he slammed the front door closed, with him on the other side.

"Get yo' ass up," my mother ordered me as she kicked me in my side. I imagine her kick was to make sure I wasn't dead.

"Get out my house." She pushed me towards the front door. All I had on was a white t-shirt and white panties. She shoved me out the door, onto the stoop and slammed the door on me. I could remember how scared and frightened I was. It was cold. It was dark. I crouched next to the step, holding my knees in my arms. Dark shadows played tricks on me. *Please someone help me*, I silently screamed. I dare not make a sound, because I was sure that if I did, someone or *something* would surely get me.

I was jolted from my walk down memory lane by a commotion outside the window. I noticed that people were scattered about below, close to the main villa. I walked out onto the balcony, the breeze hitting my face. Some of the guests stood dazed — still confused as they looked towards the structure.

At first, I could not see what they were looking at, but it only took a short amount of time before it became very clear exactly what it was that had their attention. I could hear voices, mainly Charlie's. My first instinct was to run to see what the commotion was about, but reality reminded me that I was still in my wedding dress. My beautiful hair-do was now a hair- *don't* and my makeup had run down my face. I couldn't go downstairs and face the humiliation of the crowd . . . again.

I began to sob, crying my heart out, my head in my hands. What was left of my mascara had smeared about my face. I heard Charlie's voice get louder and someone suddenly yelled, "It's not worth it Charlie." I couldn't hear exactly what he was saying, but I knew he was talking to Barbara Jean.

Yes Barbara Jean. She was no longer mother to me. No mother, or one that called herself mother, could ever do what the woman who had given birth to me had just done. Charlie was becoming louder by the moment and I knew I had better check on him, as much as he cared for me, he'd surely kill her.

I wiped my face with a cold towel and checked myself in the mirror. I was going to show some dignity. I pulled back my hair, lifted my head and headed downstairs towards the commotion. As I descend the spiral staircase, the lobby of the villa was full and people stopped and stared with looks of apology, embarrassment and pity on their faces. I wanted to turn tail and run, but I kept my head high and kept walking. I envisioned that I was the only one present and made my way to Charlie. I could see him on the patio, towered over Barbara Jean and I could see fear in her face. She wanted to run away, but there was no way he was going to let her.

"I want you to crawl back under whatever rock you slithered from under and never contact Renee again . . . or else," he seethed. His face was redder than a stop sign and he had a look of sinister I'd never seen on him.

"Or else what?" My mother asked boldly when she caught a glimpse of me standing behind him. Her fear suddenly turned into sarcasm as she grimaced and placed her hands on her hips.

"Don't tempt me Barbara Jean, don't tempt me," Charlie responded.

"She's not worth it," I said to Charlie, no longer being a coward standing in his shadow. I stood in front of her glaring. She looked from me to Charlie and then to Stuart who was sitting on a bench in a nearby gazebo with his head in his hands. Barbara Jean smiled.

"You've changed nothing here," I told her as I walked closer to her, waving my index finger and wiping that gratifying smile from her face. I had stood up to her before, but never like this. Before, I had always done it in a respectful way, but I no longer respected her.

"I have something you will never have. Do you see that man over there?" I asked pointing to Stuart. "Do you see this

17

man standing right here?" I asked pointing to Charlie. "They both love me more than any one will ever love you. You know that and you can't stand it." I stood close enough to her that she could tell what toothpaste I had used earlier. "You see, you will never have the satisfaction of having that kind of love. No one will ever love you like that except for God and I'm sure even *He* is looking down shaking his head in disgust."

"Who you thank you is?" she asked me. "I made you who you is!" she shouted.

"You're pathetic," I told her. "You're a poor excuse for a mother and a human being. I am happy and there is *nothing* you can do about it. You disgust me," I told her right before I spat into her face. "You go straight to hell!" I turned away from her and walked towards Stuart. I could hear Charlie behind me.

"If you so much as think about coming near her again," Charlie said, "I'll . . . "

"You a what?" she asked with boldness.

"I'll make you wish your little pathetic life never existed," he told her. "I can make it happen. You don't want to mess with me. So I suggest you get on the next plane back to Denver."

Barbara Jean watched Charlie walk over to Stuart and me. I could see the envy in her eyes. She knew she would never know the love that surrounded me at that moment.

Chapter 3

"You've got to eat Luv," I heard Charlie say. His hot breath brushed across the back of my neck. We lay in the hammock on the patio outside my villa. I didn't respond. I looked out across the endless ocean.

"Do you really love me?" I asked not looking away from the water.

"Why would you ask me such a thing? I shouldn't even have to answer that question," he responded with disappointment. I had seen that look in his eyes several times before.

"Do you believe that I love you?" he asked.

"Perhaps. But I'm not sure why. I've sure hurt you enough times for you to turn and walk away."

"You're allowing your mother to get into your head. Besides, despite what people say, love *does* hurt. It's a part of life." I could feel tears fall onto my neck. I don't know why I had to go and ask him the silly question in the first place. I knew he was about to go back down memory lane.

"Don't do this now," I said. I couldn't bear to turn and face him. I could hear him breathing heavily. His tears were coming at a steady pace. Charlie was by far a strong man, but he knew his vulnerabilities were safe with me—that was one of the dynamics of our relationship.

"When you love someone, it doesn't matter what they do, you still love them. Even if that means you're hurt in the process. Because, no matter what happens, you always want that person to be happy. Ultimately, you hope that it's with you, but if not, whomever they are with. You stand by that person and just hope that one day you get damn lucky."

I knew he loved me. I loved him. Actually, I loved him more than anyone knew or understood. I also understood that I stood to lose a lot where Charlie was concerned . . . including my sanity. There was no possibility of us living happily ever after. Although his father adored me, his mother was a racist. And then, there were all the other challenges that interracial couples faced. I didn't want to be responsible for tearing apart anyone's family and I knew in Charlie's stubbornness, he would disown his own family if it meant being with me.

"You mean a lot to me Charlie. I hope I never lose you." I caressed his hand that rested on my shoulder.

"You need to eat something," he attempted once more.

"My throat hurts and I have a migraine. I'll just make myself a cup of chamomile tea."

"Not while I'm here," he protested.

"I have a broken heart, not a broken hand," I glared at him.

"Your stubbornness won't work in this case," he said as he disappeared into the mini villa. I turned back towards the water. What I wouldn't give to be a free spirit—just like the dolphins I had just caught a glimpse of in the ocean.

Nature called and I hated to leave this place of sanctuary, but I had to go. As I washed my hands, my reflection taunted me to look into the mirror. It was then that I realized that I still had on my wedding dress. I looked ridiculous. Pure chaos took over my mind at that moment.

I stripped down to my bustier, underwear and white thigh high stocking and put my dress and veil into the bathtub. I doused everything with alcohol I had retrieved from the medicine cabinet. I walked back into the bedroom and looked for something to kill my pain *and* my past. I spotted an antique lighter on top of the fireplace mantle. I returned to the bathroom and set the items in the tub on fire. I watched parts of my past, *and* my future, go up in flames. My tear ducts forecasted another thunderstorm and I began to cry uncontrollably.

I looked blankly at the blurriness of the flames as I pictured Barbara Jean and Stuart in compromising positions. No matter what I did, the visions would not go away. The ominous thing about it was, Barbara Jean was staring right at me laughing hysterically like Cruella Deville.

"Bitch!" I yelled. "I hate you! Why didn't you abort me?" I uncontrollably doused more alcohol on the flames until the bottle was empty.

The smoke alarm brought me back to reality and alerted Charlie, who came running with a fire extinguisher. He sprayed the flames until not a flicker was left burning, only dark smoke billowing from the burnt fabric.

He picked me up and carried me to the adjoining room in the mini villa. He laid me on the bed and stood over me for a moment. The look in his eyes scared me. I closed mine trying to hide from his fury. When I opened them, Charlie was gone.

I grabbed a throw from a nearby chair and wrapped it around my body. I wondered where Charlie had gone. I didn't want to be alone. I threw on a sundress that I had packed. I went into the hallway of the main villa, looked over the balcony, and saw Charlie sitting in the foyer. He had his head in his lap mumbling to himself.

I knew he was hurting. I had done everything to push him away and now it was tearing him apart. I didn't want to lose him. I just didn't know how to handle my current situation. I didn't know how to deal with what had happened. Actually, I didn't want to deal with anything. I had lost Stuart and I certainly didn't want to lose Charlie.

Even though there were patrons walking about the lobby, I hauled myself down the staircase and sat on his lap. He put his arms around me, pulled me close to him and kissed the top of my head. We both sat in silence, as he rubbed my arm, as if he was coddling a teething baby who needed comfort.

"I'm sorry for pushing you away Chuck, but I don't know how to deal with this. This was supposed to be the happiest day of my life. I'm supposed to be on my honeymoon right now. That bitch has managed to take away everything from me."

"I'm still here," was all he said.

"And I still don't understand why." I just didn't know when to shut up did I?

Charlie got up and disappeared into a nearby banquet room. I put my head down. A few moments later, he returned with a cup of chamomile tea with two lemon wedges on the side of the teacup.

"Take these," he said giving me three Tylenol. "You don't have to deal with this right now. But, you *will* have to deal with it soon. The Renee I know always bounces back. And although I can't compare this to anything else that you've ever gone through, what happened upstairs really concerns me."

"Temporary insanity."

"Scary."

"For you or me?"

"Both," he said. I thought for a minute. I did go a little overboard, but no one can control pain . . . *or* temporary insanity.

"Make you think any less of me?" I asked him.

"Nope."

"I have so many questions that have no answers."

"Such as?"

"Well from what I understand, my father was in the military and he and Barbara Jean had a one night stand." I bit my lip for a moment. "A lot of things just don't add up."

22

"Well you know, we can find out whatever it is that you need to know."

"I mean, will it really matter if he's my father or not?" I asked not acknowledging anything Charlie had just said. "The point is that they slept together. It doesn't matter if it was five years or twenty years *or* thirty years ago."

Once we were back in the confines of our mini-villa, Charlie opened his cell phone and started to dial.

"Larry! How's Mary?"

Silence.

"And the children?"

Silence.

"Oh I bet he's about sick of Harvard now isn't he?"

Silence.

"You don't say?"

Silence.

"I need a favor from you."

Silence.

"See what you can come up with on a Stuart Humphries . . ."

Silence.

"Yes, that's the one. And while you're at it, see what you can come up with on a Barbara Jean Jackson. Date of birth, three, twenty, forty nine." I looked up at Charlie in terror and wondered what was he up to?

"As soon as you can."

Silence.

"Tell Mary to expect a bottle of Grenache to be delivered soon."

Silence.

"Spain?"

Silence.

"Then tell her to expect Palomero."

Silence.

"Sure thing. She's sitting right here. I'll tell her you said hello. I'll talk to you soon buddy." Charlie hung up the phone.

"What the hell was that all about?" I asked him.

"You wanted answers, and answers you shall get." Part of me hated the way Charlie threw around his power—except when I needed it. I guess I needed it now too. I stood to walk into the kitchenette.

"Unfriggin' believable," I mumbled to myself. I thought about what had transpired earlier. I couldn't quite wrap my head around it.

"I want to go away for a few days," I said in the midst of my thoughts.

"Where do you want to go?" he asked.

"Anywhere but home. Too many memories right now."

"You want head up to Frisco?" I had to think about it for a moment. I didn't want to fall vulnerable prey to Charlie. I shook that notion when I thought I could very easily be vulnerable just about anywhere.

"Sure," I answered.

He must have sensed the hesitancy in my voice because he said, "We could go to New York for a couple of days." I had never been to New York. Actually, before now, I never really had a desire to visit either.

"How about we go to New York, *then* back to Frisco?"

"Whatever you want."

"I hope I'm not inconveniencing you Charlie," I said. He looked at me, rolled his eyes and didn't say a word.

I leaned over and kissed him on his ear lobe. He backed away. *Rejection.* He saw it in my eyes. "Don't give me that look. You know I find you irresistible but I think now is hardly the time for me to take advantage of you."

"What if I want you to?" I asked with an aura of cockiness.

"You don't."

"Don't tell me what I don't want."

For the first time I that I could remember, Charlie looked in my eye with a firmness that turned me on. He said, "I said you don't and this conversation is over."

"Damn," I said. I looked at him and knew he meant business. I decided to lie down. I got halfway the bed and realized that he was right on my heels. I stopped and turned to look at him.

"Don't want another repeat," he said referring to the burning tub incident. I shook my head and continued on.

Chapter 4

I lay in bed staring at the ceiling. Today I would find out about my past as well as my future. I wasn't sure what I'd do either way. If Stuart *was* my father, I wouldn't be able to look at him. I wouldn't be able to look at myself. If Stuart *wasn't* my father, I still wouldn't be able to be with him. The fact remained that some time, long ago, he had an intimate relationship with my mother and there was no way that *we* could happen. I wondered how Stuart was feeling. I knew he had to be falling apart.

The look on his face when he saw Barbara Jean move her portly frame to the front row during our wedding spoke volumes. It was almost as if he had seen a ghost. My thoughts quickly turned to Barbara Jean. I was so angry with her that I wanted to do more than spit in her face. This was the last straw. Barbara Jean had pulled off the ultimate betrayal and there was no forgiving her.

I was faced with numerous questions and my life could not go on without those answers.

I looked over at Charlie. He was sound asleep. I retrieved my cell phone from the nightstand and dialed Stuart's number.

"You should be sleeping," he said without saying hello.

"I need to know," I said speaking low as not to wake Charlie.

"Do you really want to do this right now?"

"Yes."

Stuart explained to me that he had dated my mother in high school. He said that all the guys in school wanted to date Barbara Jean but he was the lucky one.

"We were doing good, but then Barbara Jean disappeared a couple of months before the end of the school year." I listened attentively waiting for him to get the part where he had slept with my mother.

"There were rumors going around that her father had attacked her and raped her. I tried reaching out to her but her father wouldn't let me speak to her. I would ask her sisters and brothers at school about her and they would only tell me if I knew what was best for me, I'd stay away from her. I even went by her house once, but her father chased me away with his shot gun."

Go ahead and get to the point I thought to myself.

I couldn't take it, but I allowed him to continue. "The last time I saw her was the day I was leaving for college. She was walking down the road away from my house. I called for her but she didn't hear me and I felt there was no use in going after her. I was going to break it off with her. I was leaving and chances were I wasn't going to see her again. I guess I was a coward, instead of telling her face to face, I let it end the way it did."

I decided to get to the point. "So where in all this did you sleep with my mother?" I asked defensively.

"We were dating Renee. It was in the sixties before you were even born. You make it seem like this is my fault."

"I'm sorry," I apologized. I didn't have a right taking it out on Stuart. It *was* before I was born and he had no idea that my mother and I were connected. I mean, I never once showed him a picture of my mother and there weren't too many times that I had talked about her with Stuart. I told him a little about my past, but most of the time, I tried to dodge the subject of my mother whenever it came up.

"You know, either way this turns out, we can't be together, right?" I asked.

"Yes. I know and it kills me every time I think about it." We were both on the same page but in my heart, I didn't want to erase Stuart from my life.

"I don't want to lose you Renee. Do you think we can still at least be friends? I mean after all this is over and the air clears, do you think you'll be able to accept me in your life?" I laughed for a moment. The irony of his comment mimicked my feelings, but I had no answers for him—not right now.

"I don't want to lose you either, but I need time. I just need some time." We talked a few minutes more and agreed that we'd see each other at the doctor's office later that morning.

"I love you," he said. I didn't return the sentiment and hung up the phone.

I noticed Charlie's snoring had subsided. I looked over at him. He was looking at me with remorse in his eyes.

"How long have you been awake?" I asked.

"I've been watching you for a few moments. Are you okay?" Of *course* I wasn't okay. I looked into his eyes. I could see his longing to want to make all of my problems disappear, yet he felt so helpless.

"No, I'm not alright and not even *you* can make this go away."

Charlie sat up in the bed next to me and took me into his arms. He kissed me on my forehead.

"Even if I could make it go away, somehow I don't think you'd feel any better."

"You can't fix all of my problems."

"I sure would like to," he mumbled.

"What am I going to do Charlie?"

"Let's wait to see how things go with the test results first. Then *together* we will search and find the answers." My alter ego slapped me on my shoulder.

Had you accepted Charlie's proposal in the first place you wouldn't be going through all this drama.

I knew *it* was right. Charlie had stood by me through thick and thin. I wasn't even sure *why* he stayed. I shot down his advances time after time. I knew that he would die for me if need be. What was I thinking even getting involved with Stuart? A love like Charlie's rarely came in one's lifetime. I took a moment to search within.

What was wrong with me? Had my mother had me so bound, that I couldn't even use common sense?

In the back of my mind, I could hear Charlie mumbling something but I was so heavy into my thoughts I couldn't hear what he was saying. He got my attention when he got out of bed and walked into the bathroom slamming the door. I knew he was hurting and I knew what he was thinking. He was thinking the same thing my alter ego had just confirmed. Nevertheless, he had to understand what I had just gone through. My life had just been pulled from underneath my feet. I didn't think he was being fair. He chose to stay with me, even though he knew I loved Stuart.

Sometimes I felt like just walking away from Charlie so that he could move on with his life, but I knew better. There is no way he would let me. And, even knowing that, I knew I didn't deserve him.

I got out of bed and knocked on the bathroom door . . . no answer. I knocked again, calling out to Charlie . . . again, no answer. I opened the door. Charlie sat on the chaise lounge that was near the large picture window. He wasn't doing anything in particular, just heavy in thought.

"Charlie," I said.

"I'm fine," was all he said. I kneeled down in front of him, both my hands placed on his knees and looked up into his eyes.

"Please don't shut me out. You have to understand what I'm going through right now," I pleaded. He still refused to speak, so I felt rather than badger him, I'd give him his space.

I wanted to get dressed and get to the doctor's office before Stuart got there. I needed answers and wanted to put this part of my life behind me. I showered and dressed in a black pantsuit and a white tank top. When I was finished, Charlie was waiting in the kitchenette with a cup of coffee as a peace offering.

He had ordered a fruit tray from room service. I declined, telling him that I didn't know if I should eat anything before the test. Charlie argued that the doctor would be testing DNA not for diabetes. I laughed but still didn't take the coffee or fruit. I was too nervous and the coffee would only make it worse. I rushed Charlie along with his breakfast and we scurried out the door.

When Charlie and I arrived at Dr. Chow's office, Stuart was already there. He looked as if he had spent the night there. His face had aged at least ten years. My heart sunk. I didn't know what to do or what to say. What I did next surprised even myself. I sat down next to him and took his hand in mine.

"No matter what happens, we're going to be alright," I said giving him a comforting squeeze.

"Easy for you to say," he said looking at me for the first time since Charlie and I had walked into the doctor's office. "Either way, *my* life is over." I didn't know how to respond. How *do* you respond to something like that? I knew in a way he was right. It would be hard for either of us to go on, let alone, love again.

Dr. Chow's nurse came out to the waiting room where we were sitting. She instructed Stuart and me to follow her. Charlie offered to go with me for support but I convinced him to stay in the waiting room.

After our blood was drawn, Stuart and I were escorted back to the waiting room. Soon after, Dr. Chow appeared.

"We should have your test results back by Wednesday," he said.

"That long huh?" Stuart asked.

"I know it seems like a lifetime, but its only two days. I will call you both and we'll meet you back here at that time."

† † †

The next two days were hell for me. My stress level was at an extreme and I could not eat or sleep. As a matter of fact, anything that I tried to eat found its way back up. Come to think of it, my period was over two and a half weeks late. I shook the notion that I was pregnant and chalked it up to stress. It wasn't the first time that my period was late, and usually stress was the culprit.

I tried to make sense of my life and wondered what I would do after the test results were given. Would I go on with my life and never have contact with Stuart again? Would we be friends? If he *was* my father, how would I transition from being lover to daughter? Would I transition at all? The thought made me ill.

Maybe I should move somewhere far away. Start my life over, somewhere where no one knew me. Perhaps I could go somewhere where no one would know the secret that my mother had revealed at the altar. I knew I would never forgive

Barbara Jean and knew I would *never* have a relationship with her. All my life I had yearned for a relationship with her, but now, I wanted her to disappear. I no longer wanted any association with her. She was dead to me.

The butterflies in my stomach began to dance again. I ran toward the bathroom but I was too late. I had thrown up on the floor. Charlie was nowhere to be found. I was somewhat relieved. I didn't want him fussing over me. I washed my face and cleaned up the mess I had left on the floor. I lay down for a moment to try to stabilize my dizziness. After a while, the nausea subsided.

The room was quiet, not a soul stirring. I straightened my hair and went downstairs to the lobby. I didn't see Charlie in the foyer, the lobby or the lounge. I wasn't sure where he had gone, but I knew it wouldn't be long before he'd be back. I walked out to the garden—the very place where my life had changed forever. The chairs, flowers and decorations were still in their place. The altar where I was supposed to become Mrs. Stuart Humphries was still intact.

I sat on one of the chairs in the front row, stared towards the beach and thought about the beauty, the love and excitement I had felt just days before. I envisioned myself walking down the aisle with Charlie as he delivered me to my husband to be. I imagined Stuart and I saying our vows to each other and the preacher pronouncing us husband and wife, our first kiss, our first dance.

We would jump the broom and exit the garden as our family and friends threw rice and confetti at us chanting *Mr. and Mrs. Humphries*! We would go on our honeymoon and make love over and over. We would later have children, get a dog, and grow old together. And now, all that was gone. In an instant, my life had changed and I had no idea how I would recover.

I was so lost in thought that I didn't hear Charlie walk into the garden. He sat in the chair behind me and rubbed my shoulders. He didn't say anything—I gathered there was really nothing to say. No words needed to be wasted. I broke out in tears and for the first time, Charlie didn't run to my rescue. He didn't attempt to console me. I had to wonder if I was losing both the men in my life—the two people that I knew for sure, loved me.

My thoughts were interrupted again, by nausea, then vomit. I made a dash for the lobby, but again, didn't make it. This time, Charlie escorted me into the villa and up to our room.

† † †

Dr. Chow's nurse called to let me know that our DNA results had come back and wanted to meet with Stuart and I. The vomiting would not subside no matter what I did. Regardless, nothing was going to stop me from going to Dr. Chow's office and finding out the results of those tests.

You okay?" Stuart asked me when we got to the doctor's office.

"I'll be fine," I answered.

Dr. Chow's nurse came into the waiting room and escorted Stuart and I to the doctor's office. This time Charlie followed. I wasn't in any condition to interject.

"Well, I have the results of your DNA test," Dr. Chow said as he shook everyone's hand. He gestured for us to have a seat in the chairs seated in front of his desk. Before he proceeded to give us the results, he explained to us how the test determined paternity and a few of the scientific facts that surrounded the test. I didn't want to hear all of that, so I rushed him along.

"The results doctor," I said sharply.

"The tests show a 99.9% accuracy . . ." he paused looking from me to Stuart then to Charlie. I shifted in my seat as he continued. "Stuart is *not* your father Renee."

I couldn't shake my gaze from Stuart but he still wouldn't look my way. Even so, I could see the tears running down his cheeks. He looked cold and lifeless . . . zombielike.

I noticed the tear that barely escaped Charlie's eye. He wiped away any trace of it before it could reach his cheek. I wasn't sure if his tear, was a tear of joy or a tear of sadness that I had lost the love of my life. There was a long moment of silence in the room.

"I think we all need a break right about now. Stuart, Renee and I are going to be in New York for a few days. After that we'll go back to San Francisco until she can or until she *wants* to go back home. Eventually, you two need to sort this out. I know this can't be easy for either of you."

Stuart extended his hand to Charlie, but Charlie pulled him in for a long embrace. Charlie told Stuart that things would work out the way they were supposed to, whatever way that was.

I couldn't leave Stuart there without hugging him. I sunk my tear soaked face into his chest. I was reminded of how safe I felt when I was in his arms. The scent of his cologne reminded me of our passion. The feel of his body gelling into mine, reminded me of how we could see into each other's souls. I inhaled him and didn't want to let him go, but I knew I had to. The more I thought about it, the more cheated I felt, and the angrier I became.

"You know, I want to know why she did this," I blurted out. I still loved Stuart. I wasn't going to deny that. I wanted to know why Barbara Jean had made it impossible for us to be together.

"You don't need to do this. Not now," Stuart said. "Would it matter? Would it make a difference? Would it change the fact that I can't be with the only woman I ever loved? My soul mate?"

"My wanting to know has nothing to do with you at this point," I told Stuart. "This is between Barbara Jean and me now. I want to know why she had to wait until my wedding. I want to know the reasons why a mother would do this to her own daughter. I want to know why she is so hateful!" I was so loud that the nurse came to see if everything was all right. I apologized to her and made my way out to Charlie's car. Charlie and Stuart followed me.

"He's right Luv, you don't need to deal with this right now."

"I need you to stop trying to protect me," I snapped at Charlie. "I'm not a fucking baby!" He held his hands up in retreat and stepped back.

"I want to go see her now! And, either one of you is going to take me, or I'm going by myself. Either way, I'm going." I was furious now. I was mad as hell. Mad at Charlie, mad at Stuart, mad at my mother, mad at myself and mad at God.

For nearly thirty-two years, I had endured heartache and pain, and I was always told that God was just testing me. When was God going to stop testing me and cut me a break? When was he going to see that my spirit could take no more? When would God see that *He* had broken my heart?

"Well if you're going, I'm going with you," Stuart told me. We piled into our cars and headed to Barbara Jean's hotel. Stuart followed

I dialed Marlene's cell number. "Hello?"

"When are you leaving to go back to Denver?" I asked her without any formalities. As far as I was concerned, she too was dead to me. She was silent for a moment.

"Answer me you bitch," I yelled. "You at least owe me that."

"Tomorrow at four," Marlene finally answered. After all I had done for her, she knew she owed it to me. I was there for Marlene when even her own parents didn't want anything to do with her. I was there to pick her up when she was down, there to loan her money when she didn't have a dime, nursed her through two abortions and the countless times she was beaten or humiliated by a man she swore she couldn't live without. She knew that she hadn't been a good friend to me and she knew that she would never get the chance to redeem herself.

"Where is she staying?"

"Holiday Inn by the airport. Room 217," she said before hanging up the phone.

Moments later, I knocked on Barbara Jean's hotel door. Without investigation, she opened the door. I was actually shocked that Marlene hadn't alerted her of my unwelcomed visit.

"What tha hell you doin' hea'?" I had caught her off guard, but she changed her persona when she saw Stuart and Charlie standing behind me. "I see you brought yo' boyfriend and yo' molestin' daddy," she seethed.

"You know, I really would like to know what you planned on gaining by pulling that stunt you pulled," I told her, barging into her room.

"You never knew who yo' father was, now you do," Barbara Jean smirked. "I felt it was my civil duty to let you know."

Ignorant I thought to myself.

"You're lying! You can't tell me that was the only reason for your fowl attempt to ruin my life. You didn't know Stuart and I were engaged until I sent you the wedding invitation.

You haven't seen or heard from Stuart since the day he left for college." I thought about it for a moment. I had sent her an invitation and it did have Stuart's name on it. However, it still didn't matter. There was no excuse for what she had done.

"I done been knowin' 'bout you and him for a while. Marlene sent me a pic'cha of him when you leff me and moved to San Diego." My nerves were in overdrive. Barbara Jean turned away from me. I didn't know what Marlene's intentions were for doing what she did, but at this point, I didn't care. I was done with them both.

"I'm done with you Barbara Jean. I spent all my life trying to live up to your expectations, to get your approval and to get you to love me but it was never enough. All you've done is hurt me time after time. What have I ever done to you? Why do you hate me so much?" She just looked at me, no response at all.

"You've ruined our lives," Stuart chimed in.

"Oh shut tha hell up Stuart. You ain't thank 'bout ruinin' nobodies life when you left me pregnant and went off to that high siditty school. I had Renee all by myself. You wasn't there when she was born, and you sho' as hell wasn't there to help me raise her."

"That was her *father's* job," Stewart spewed.

"You is her father you bastid," she yelled. I watched the vicious banter between Stuart and Barbara Jean.

"Who else were you sleeping with Barbara Jean?" he challenged her. Charlie and I looked at her. We wanted to know the answer too.

"How dare you, you . . . you sorry son of a bitch. You was the only one I was wit'. I was young and you took advan'age of me."

Stuart laughed hysterically. "I can't take any more of this bullshit. Renee, we'll work this out baby girl. Know this right here right now, no matter what this poor excuse of a woman has tried to do, I will always love you. She can't take that away from us." Barbara Jean looked at Stuart in shock but then started to cry.

"Charlie, I will give you a call. I'm out of here." He kissed me on my forehead and with that, Stuart disappeared onto the other side of the door.

"Tha's right, walk out. You good at it," she yelled towards the door. I stood there with my arms crossed looking at my poor wretched excuse of a mother. Even though I was disgusted with her, and I pitied her. I felt sorry for her because even after fifty years, she still didn't get it. However, that didn't change the fact that I wanted nothing else to do with her.

"You're so sad," I said. "So sad and pitiful."

"I did you a favor," Barbara Jean said.

"Stuart is not my father," I said looking to see her expression.

"He *is* yo father. Anyone can see the 'semblance."

I shook my head and let out a sigh. "Like I said, I'm done. I'm done here. I'm done with you. You didn't win. You've done such a good job trying. I almost feel for you. *Almost.*"

"This the thanks I get for preventin' you from marryin' yo' own daddy?" Barbara Jean said in all her audacity. I threw the test results at her.

"Charlie, please take me home." Charlie put his arm around me and escorted me outside, but he stopped once outside the doorframe and turned around.

"I hope you remember what I told you. If you come near her again, you *will* be sorry," With that, Barbara Jean slammed the door in our faces.

Chapter 5

As planned, Charlie and I flew to New York for a few days. It was a sight to see and I enjoyed the time we spent there, but it was as I thought it would be and I was still sure that I never wanted to live there.

After we left New York, we headed to San Francisco. I had always felt comfortable in Charlie's home, but there was nothing like being in your own home.

I had allowed Barbara Jean enough airtime and space in my life and now it was time to disconnect. I had to get things back to normal. I decided that it was also time to stop leaning on Charlie. It was time for me to go back to San Diego, back to my home, back to work and what was left of my life.

Charlie was insistent on staying with me so I made a deal with him. I told him he could stay through the weekend, but when I came home from work that Monday, he needed to be gone. I didn't mean to be so harsh, but at the time, that was the only thing he understood.

When we landed in San Diego, I was somewhat relieved. San Francisco was okay, but San Diego was where I felt peace and serenity. It was where I felt most comfortable and most of all, it felt like home to me.

As usual, Charlie had a car waiting at the airport to take us back to my place. When we drove up the front driveway, I sighed . . . in relief *and* sadness. It was time to put my big girl panties on and do what I had to do.

Even though the alarm was armed, Charlie went in first to make sure everything was secured. Once he gave the okay, I went in looking around. Everywhere I looked, I saw Stuart. I laid my purse on the table in the foyer and headed to my office. I could hear my answering machine beep before I got to the door.

My office was probably the only room that I didn't see Stuart in. I powered up my computer system and checked my messages. There were several messages from clients and vendors and one from Stuart. I didn't know what part of the house Charlie was in so I turned the volume down and listened to the message.

"Hey baby. Uh, I mean . . . Renee. Hell, what am I saying? You are my baby. You will always be my baby. I wanted to apologize for everything . . . for all of this. I wish things were different thirty years ago, just like I wished they were different now. But, neither of us can change the past. We *can* change our future. I guess what I'm trying to say is, I don't care about anything or anyone but you. Since we left Barbara . . . " He coughed.

"Since we left there, I haven't been able to eat or sleep and I can't stop thinking about you. Renee, I can't breathe and I don't want to live without you. So I guess . . . I guess what I am trying to say is . . . I still want to be your husband. I know. I know. It's too soon. That's why I didn't call the house number or your cell number. But, when you finally get this . . . well . . . That's what I wanted you to know. I love you. I love you with all my heart. Oh God, do I love you." With that, he let out a deep sigh the phone went dead.

I wasn't aware of the tears that were streaming down my face and soaking a stack of papers that lay on my desk. Nor did I notice Charlie standing in the doorway. I looked up. He gave me those puppy dog eyes and disappeared again. I didn't have time for his ego, so I let him be.

I was exhausted. Barbara Jean had taken all my energy and I needed to be rejuvenated. My mind wandered to Stuart once more. We were both hurting but that did not stop us from loving one another. I wondered what he was doing, where he was, what he had on. Had he eaten? Was he taking care of himself? I would have to see him eventually . . . we worked for the same company.

I thought for a moment about the whole ordeal. Barbara Jean and Stuart had a relationship well over thirty years ago and tests had proven that he and I were not related. You can't help who you fall in love with, right? All I knew was I still loved that man. I still wanted him and I wasn't ready to let him go. Did I have to? I know there are some places one should not go and lines one should not cross. A mother and a daughter should never share a man, *ever*. But, in our defense, neither of us knew before we fell in love and it *was* a lifetime ago.

I sat down and leaned my head against my chair. I closed my eyes and tried to rationalize the entire situation.

† † †

I heard the doorbell ring and looked at the clock next to my bed. It was six o'clock in the evening. I didn't quite remember lying down and had no idea if Charlie was still around. I threw on a black satin robe that I had purchased from Victoria's Secret and descended the stairs to answer the door. I could see a silhouette in the stained glass. It was Stuart.

"Did you lose your key?" I asked after opening the door.

"No. I actually came to return it and I didn't want to intrude." I looked at Stuart for a minute—*and* like he was crazy. I was sure he hadn't gotten any sleep since the Barbara Jean debacle. I allowed him to enter and shut the door. I began climbing the staircase but stopped and turned around to find him standing where I had left him.

"Are you going to just stand there or are you coming?" I asked and then proceeded up the staircase. This time I could hear his footsteps behind me.

I found refuge once more in my king sized bed. Stuart removed his shoes and I patted the empty side of the bed. He removed his shirt, something that was more of a habit than anything. He got under the covers next to me. And just as natural as breathing, I laid my head on his bare chest. I loved the way he smelled. The aroma of Issey Miyake filled my nostrils.

Before I knew it, Stuart was snoring away. I rubbed his chest and played with the patch of hair on this chest that trailed from the middle of his chest and disappeared under his slacks. Tears fell from my eyes onto his chest. He rubbed my arm and kissed my forehead. We lay together, loving on each other with our minds and our hearts . . . without words . . . without any sexual innuendos, just love from our hearts. Before long, we were both sound asleep.

It was after midnight when I woke up. I was thirsty and had to go to the bathroom. I had been going a lot lately, but I figured it was due to the amount of stress I was under. I smiled at Stuart. He was still sleeping.

When I came out of the bathroom, Stuart wasn't in bed. I heard the water running in the bathroom, down the hallway.

I wondered where Charlie was. I hadn't seen him for a while. Since he had a key to my house, I didn't give it too much thought.

"Are you hungry?" I asked Stuart hanging onto the frame of the bathroom door.

"A little. But you shouldn't be eating this late, you're getting a little thick around the waist," he smirked as he wrapped his strong arms around my waist. He pulled me close. I was lost in love. I inhaled him and looked up at him.

I broke his embrace and went to the guest room to see if Charlie was still there. His things were not there. I went back to my bedroom and checked my cell phone. He had sent me a text.

You two needed to be alone, so I'm staying at a hotel tonight. Talk to you soon. Luv you!

It was obvious that Charlie had walked in on Stuart and me last night. I took in a deep breath. I would deal with Charlie later. As for now, Stuart and I had some things to work out. If I knew Charlie, he would always be there.

"You know we need to talk, right?" I asked Stuart after I took my mind off Charlie.

He nodded and escorted me down the staircase and into the kitchen. I decided since it was late, I'd make a salad. I put a few pieces of bacon in a pan and put on a pot of water for hard-boiled eggs. I poured Romaine lettuce and spinach in a bowl with corn and black beans, tomatoes, red onions, cucumbers and feta cheese. I crumbled the eggs and bacon and topped it off with a safflower oil, vinegar, and garlic pepper mixture.

"I love your salads," he said.

"I know," I said and sat beside him.

"I can't imagine my life without you," I said in between bites. He continued eating and nodded. "Do you think we can look past the obvious?" I asked. He nodded again, eating as if it was his last meal. I walked around the kitchen island and retrieved two SoBe drinks from the fridge and gave him the Zen Blend.

"Do you *want* to get past this?" I asked. He nodded. I stopped in mid-chew, "Do you still love me?"

This time, he stopped chewing and gazed into my eyes. "More than my own life," he finally spoke. I was touched by his endearment. We both continued chewing. Stuart had always been the strong silent type, except when he was pursuing me. I liked him either way.

"So where do we go from here?"

"That's up to you. You already know what I want and how I feel."

"And you doubt my feelings for you?"

He shrugged. "No, not at all. But I know this is difficult for you."

"And it's not for you?"

"Nope," he said smacking his lips and taking a drink of his SoBe. "It was at first, but not anymore." Nice to see he could bounce back so easily. "If I could marry you right this minute I would. If I could make love to you, right this minute, I would."

I blushed and turned away from him.

He sat his drink down and turned to me. "Do you realize how hard it has been this last week? Wanting to hold you, just to touch you?"

"What's stopping you?" I asked with a bit of irritation. Truth be told I was feeling the same way.

"The way you looked at me when Barbara Jean pulled her little stunt. It was a look of disgust and disdain. It was as if you thought I was a disease or something and I was sure at that moment I had lost you."

"You're giving up on me?"

"Never. I wanted to give you a little space."

"And how do you feel at this moment?" I asked him.

"I can't even begin to describe how I'm feeling right now."

"Then show me," I told him.

He paused and looked at me. I raised my eyebrow to make sure he knew exactly how I felt. He picked me up and took me to the sofa in the great room.

"You know Charlie has a key," I said.

"Yeah, we need to talk about that." He carried me up the staircase and into my bedroom and locked the door behind us.

As I sat on the bed, he stood with his back against the door. He looked at me for a few moments and I thought he was going to change his mind and then he said, "Not like this."

"What?" I asked.

"I don't think we should make love. Not like this."

"You're crazy. Got me all hot and bothered over here and my hormones going crazy. You better get over here."

"I'm serious. I think we should wait until we get married. That is if you still want to go that route." I rolled my eyes at him, laid back on the bed and covered my face with a pillow. He was right. We should do it the right way.

"God don't bless no mess," I mumbled. "Can you at least hold me?" I playfully whined. He laughed and dove onto the bed. We tussled around for a few moments. We were intimate without the sex and it felt good. I massaged his arms and shoulders while he massaged my scalp. I was in pure ecstasy.

In mid-moan, he blurted out, "Will you . . . marry me . . . again?"

"Yes," I answered without giving it a second thought. "And this time, no one will stop us." He kissed me passionately and we fell asleep.

Chapter 6

I woke up the next morning rushing for the toilet, nearly missing it.

"Are you alright?" Stuart asked from the bathroom door. This nausea had become a nuisance.

Nerves my foot. Something else was going on.

"Throwing up, always thirsty, always going to the bathroom . . . You're pregnant," he said.

"Now you're a doctor?" I asked splashing cold water on my face.

"No but I know enough to know that my wifey is pregnant." The sound of that made me smile.

"Future wifey and I'm not pregnant," I refuted.

"Okay, but we need to get you to a doctor."

"Look at you already throwing around your husbandly authority." We both laughed.

He turned serious. "In your own time, you need to have a talk with Charlie."

I knew he was right. Although I knew he wanted me happy, I knew Charlie wasn't going to be too thrilled to know that Stuart and I were going to follow through with our marriage. And, if what Stuart said was true, Charlie wouldn't be too thrilled knowing I might be pregnant either. There was just too much going on in my life.

"I want to let him down as easily as possible."

"I can respect that. I know he means a lot to you, but don't wait too long. Hey, if it makes you feel better, he can be our children's godfather." That part surprised me. "I'd never put you in a position where you'd have to end your friendship," he added. "Just as long as he knows who the head honcho is."

I knew what Stuart meant. Although Charlie and I had not been intimate since long before Stuart and I became engaged, I knew it made Stuart feel uncomfortable when Charlie parked in my bed at night. He knew nothing went on but he was a man—territorial and he knew Charlie wasn't letting me go without a fight.

"Just give me some time," I said. He nodded and kissed me on the forehead.

"I need to go by my place, get showered and go into the office for a bit," he said. Stuart had a good supply of clothes in my closet but I knew him well enough to know this was his way of saying he needed his space.

"Make that appointment for the pregnancy test," he yelled from the front door.

Just as I reached the catwalk and looked over the banister, Charlie walked through the door, looking like a deer caught in headlights. He and Stuart shook hands and traded pleasantries, and then Stuart headed out the door as Charlie shut it behind him.

We gazed at each other for a moment and then he finally asked, "Should I even ask?"

"Are you hungry?" I asked him as I came down the stairs. I knew this was going to be hard and figured I might as well tell him on a full stomach—perhaps he'd take it better that way.

Right?

"Not particularly," he answered. He made his way to the mini bar and fixed himself a drink instead. I opened the fridge to see what was in it. I hadn't done any grocery shopping in a while. The fridge was bare. I settled on a can of albacore tuna and a box of Triscuits.

Charlie and I retreated to the sofa in the great room in front of the television. He parked the channel on CNN.

"So," he said, more in question form than a statement. "Are you going to tell me what I walked in on?" I took a few deep breaths and paused for a bit.

Once the butterflies settled in the pit of my stomach, I finally spoke.

"Stuart and I have decided to go ahead with the marriage."

Charlie diverted his attention from CNN to me. His face was beet red. "I see," he said. He stared at me with his puppy dog eyes.

"Don't look at me like that Charlie. Just because Barbara Jean ruined our wedding doesn't mean I stopped loving him." I defended myself.

"I know. It's just so soon. When did you two come to this conclusion?"

"Last night" I said not looking him in the eye. I knew he was going to jump to conclusions. He stood up and began pacing back and forth in front of the television.

"Last night?" he asked. "Hmmm. Was that before or after . . ."

"Don't do that Charlie," I interrupted him. "That's not fair."

"I just have to wonder if you were thinking clearly Luv, that's all."

I put my feet up on the cocktail table. I wasn't going to divulge that Stuart and I hadn't made love since the disaster, but even if we had, it wasn't his business. "Charlie you know I love you."

"Yes, I know."

"And, you know I love Stuart."

"Yes. I'm reminded of that every day."

"I'm being honest with you."

"I know, I know. I guess in the back of my mind I knew that it would come to this. I just hoped that I was wrong.

"Mr. Thatcher. I thought you wanted me to be happy." He sat down next to me and took me in his arms.

"I do Luv. Really I do. Stuart's a swell guy and all. I just hoped he'd . . . like . . . disappear. "

"Charles Thatcher!' I exclaimed.

"Seriously, I just want to be in your life forever."

"And you will be. As a matter of fact, it was Stuart's idea for you to be our children's godfather."

Charlie raised his eyebrows. "Children?' he released me and waited for an explanation. I put my head down. I didn't want to see the look on his face.

"I might be pregnant." I said.

"Whoa!" he said standing up.

"Pregnant but . . . when . . . how?"

"You're kidding me right?"

Charlie grew more upset by the moment. I knew the best thing to do was to give him space. He made a beehive for the door and slammed it on the way out. Tears welled up in my eyes and began flowing like a river. I finally called on the one person that I seemed to have forgotten about during this entire ordeal. I got on my knees, kneeled over the cocktail table, and began to pray. I prayed to my God, to Jesus, for strength, guidance and discernment. I begged for forgiveness and mercy. I cried, prayed and *snotted* for what seemed like hours.

After I made a breakthrough, I headed upstairs to take a shower and then called the office. I let my secretary know that I would be in sometime that week. I needed to see if I could get in to see Dr. Chow. Luckily, I was able to get in that afternoon.

I was so pleased with the evolution of technology. Although the entire process took two hours, I had the results of my pregnancy test before I left Kaiser Permanente. Even though I was nervous, and downright scared, I knew Stuart would be elated to know he was going to be a father in about five months or so. I wanted to surprise him.

I headed over to his house to cook dinner. I let myself in and laid my purse and day planner on a table in the foyer. I saw Stuart sitting in a wing back chair in his living room as I headed towards the kitchen.

"What's wrong babe?" I asked him. "I thought you were going to work."

"I stopped by for a few minutes, but my head wasn't in it, so I came home." I sat on his lap and dried the tears from his chocolate face.

"Talk to me," I said.

He squeezed me tightly. "I had to pray. I know God did not put you in my life just to take you away. I had to thank him. I was so scared." I took his head onto my bosom and kissed his head, his ears, his nose and then his lips. We held each other for a while . . . again with no words.

"Don't squeeze me too tight," I finally said. "This rascal might pop out before it's supposed to."

Stuart froze for a moment looking at my swollen belly. I found it a bit tickling that he had noticed my expanding waistline, as he had put it, before I had. He looked up at me with question in his eyes. I nodded confirming.

"You went today?" he asked. I nodded. "When?"

"In about five months?" I answered knowing what he meant. He picked me up and turned me around, and before I could tell him to stop, I had vomited on us *both*.

"You're so nasty," he teased. He carried me to his shower, stripping clothes from my body, piece by piece. After we showered, I threw on one of his big shirts. He tried to get me into his San Diego Chargers Jersey—but there was no way that was happening.

"You know I'm not putting that anywhere on my body, so stop playing." We both laughed. He spent a lot of time trying to convince me to leave the Dallas Cowboys fandom and become a Chargers fan. I always told him, not even if hell froze over.

I sauntered into the kitchen to get dinner ready. Stuart followed me hugging me from behind.

"I'm going to be a dad," he said with excitement. It warmed my heart to see him go from sad to happy in a matter of minutes. I knew he would make an excellent father and an excellent husband.

"What are you doing?" he asked me when I started pulling out pots and pans.

"Cooking my baby dinner," I responded.

"Oh no you're not," he said with great authority.

"I'm pregnant, not disabled," I said.

"I know, but were' going out to celebrate tonight."

Who was I to kill his joy? He made reservations at one of the restaurants in the downtown Gas Lamp District.

"So what do you want?" I asked Stuart as we were seated at private table at the Hard Rock Café.

"The fajitas are to die for," he answered.

"Note to self, my future hubby just used the term, *to die for*. You've been hanging around Charlie much too long. I meant do you want a boy or a girl."

"It doesn't matter, just as long as it's healthy."

"Yeah, yeah, yeah. That's what they all say." I perused the menu and selected the Salmon Caesar salad. "I'll also have a glass of your house wine," I told the waiter as he took our order.

"Uh, she'll have iced tea," Stuart interjected. The waiter looked confused as he looked from Stuart to me. "She's pregnant," Stuart told him. The waiter smiled and gave his congratulations. I had forgotten about the pregnancy already. Silly me.

"Sorry," I apologized and smiled at Stuart. He smiled back. His smile could melt butter. I could see why Barbara Jean was so bitter. I'd be mad if a catch like Stuart got away too. *Ugh*. Why did she have to enter my head?

"We only have a few months to come up with names," he said breaking my trance. "Of course if it's a boy, my preference would be Stuart Charles Humphries."

"Wow!" I said. He amazed me more and more each day. Charlie would be thrilled to know that Stuart was willing to share his son with him.

Suddenly I got this funny thought in my head. A while ago, Stuart had teased me about being with Charlie saying he was old enough to be my grandfather and I had teased him about being old enough to be my father.

Nausea.

It wasn't so funny now.

"What? Don't you think he'd be pleased to know that although he can't have my wife, he can share a part of her?"

"Yes, that's true. But I don't know too many men, especially black men, who'd share their child with their fiancé's ex-lover and best friend. "

"Key word being *ex* and he won't always be your best friend. That's my job," he said with a sense of cockiness.

"What if it's a girl?" I asked trying to change the subject.

"I'll leave that to you, and Chuck can pick the middle name."

"I like Justice," I said.

"Justice is a nice name. It sounds like a prestigious name. Whatever you decide, just make sure our baby isn't a LaQuisha or Boomsheeka. And please don't name our baby after a car or any type of alcohol," I laughed.

"What's wrong with Boomsheeka Porscha Alize?" I asked. He didn't find that one bit funny.

"I have to wonder what goes through some parent's heads when they name their children. I mean, come on. Have you ever heard of doctor or lawyer named LaQuisha? Hell, my baby may end up being president of the United States."

He was on a roll, and then his voice changed into a deep announcer connotation. "Ladies and gentlemen, introducing the next president of the United States, President Boomquisha Hyundai Hennessey Humphries!"

I nearly spit my tea out at him. He was on a roll. Did I mention that his sense of humor was one of the many things I loved about him? I laughed so hard, I nearly peed myself.

"Stoppit! You're going to cause me to have an accident right here at this table." He obliged, looked at me and then smiled.

"You're so beautiful when you laugh. And you're practically glowing," he said. I blushed. "I love you Renee Matthews."

"I love you too Stuart Humphries."

We continued to cheese and grin at each other as we ate our dinner, and talked more about our plans for the future.

Chapter 7

I was looking at the ticker outside my office. The market was active and we were all waiting for a news conference with Alan Greenspan. He was going to reveal whether the feds were going to raise or lower interest rates. Pearl came into my office to return a few files that I had her assess.

"What's your consensus?" she asked.

"I think he's going to lower rates a quarter of a point. Then again, that's just my guess. I don't see rates going up, at least not in this market."

"I think they're going to remain the same. Markets are pretty stable, no need to disturb the masses," she said. We both walked out into the main area of our floor where eight large paneled televisions hung from the ceiling. The rest of the office joined us.

"*Pssst* . . ." Pearl said. "You need to lay off the pasta girlfriend."

How rude I thought. I gave her a stern look.

"You know I don't hold my tongue. You always come in here looking like a million bucks. Maybe it's just water retention. Lay off the salt," she said winking at me.

I scooted closer to her and whispered, "For your information, I happen to be pregnant." After I told her, I immediately put my index finger to my lips shushing her. "Keep it quiet."

"Congratulations!" she said.

"Thank you, now be quiet so I can hear Mr. Greenspan." We both laughed.

We were both wrong with our predictions. Greenspan lowered interest rates three quarters of a point. The economy was looking good.

As soon as he made that announcement, the market started going into a frenzy and our phone lines went haywire. Everyone looked like little mice running to their desks and taking orders for stocks and other securities. I looked around the office and smiled.

I returned to my desk. My message light was flashing. I pressed the speaker button and then the flashing light. I retrieved my messages and began calling back clients.

I was on a long call with a client when I saw an email come across my Outlook email client. I tried not to focus on the email but rather my client, but he wasn't interested in buying anything. He just wanted a million and one quotes. I finally interrupted him.

"Mr. Shovolotzky, I'm going to either get you to one of our quote reps or direct you to our automated system and they can give you all the quotes you'd like." He mumbled something then told me that no one gave him quotes and information that he wanted and needed and didn't want to talk to anyone else but me. He opted to go online to get the rest of his quotes. "Tell Miriam I said hello sir." We said our goodbyes and I disconnected my earpiece.

I opened my Outlook email and found an email from Charlie. He was letting me know that we were rolling out a new version of Schwab 500 for our wealthier investors. His email was strictly professional.

I responded:

Greetings Mr. Thatcher,

Thank you for giving our office the heads up. We are certain this will be a successful product and our clients will be just as excited about it as we are.

Sincerely,
R. Matthews.

I didn't have much time to nurse Charlie's bruised ego, so I threw myself into my work. In addition to what was going on in the markets, I had to catch up on what I had left behind when I took personal leave to get married. My inbox was filled with prospectuses and IPO announcements.

"These are for you," Pearl said entering my office. She had her hands full with a bouquet of white roses.

Stuart is so sweet I thought.

Much to my surprise, the roses weren't from Stuart. They were from one of my clients.

The card read:

Renee,
Much gratitude to you for making me tons of money and on your recent nuptials. I sure hope he realizes he is one lucky man."
My best,
Aaron Thompson.

"Awww, how sweet," I said aloud. I asked Pearl to send Mr. Thompson a thank you card, even though I had planned on calling him and thanking him personally. I'd leave out the part about Stuart and me not being married.

"Do you need something? You're looking a little flushed," she asked me. "As a matter of fact you don't look well at all."

"I just need to get something to eat," I said. "I didn't eat breakfast this morning."

"You can't do that any longer. You're eating for two now, and that baby's hungry. What would you like me to order you?"

"Can you have Quizno's deliver? Actually, pass the menu around the office. Lunch is on me today."

"My, aren't we feeling generous," she smirked. "In the meantime, there should be crackers in your cabinet and ginger ale in your box over there." I absolutely loved Pearl, she took extra care of me and took her job very seriously, and, you can best believe we were paying her every penny she was worth.

I hit my speakerphone and dialed Stuart's extension. "Babe. We're ordering from Quizno's."

"You want me to come to your office?"

"That would be nice," I answered.

"Give me a few moments and let Pearl know I'll have my usual."

"You've got it," she said towards the phone. She smiled and disappeared on the other side of my door.

"You doing okay," Stuart asked me once I took him off speakerphone. "Do you need anything?"

"I'm fine, just a little hungry. How's your day going my King?"

"My day is always good as long as my Queen is a part of it." I could see his smile through the phone and I was sure he could see mine.

† † †

It was eight o'clock when I finally decided to wrap things up in the office and head home. I was a bit surprised to see Charlie's car in the garage when I pressed the garage door opener. I entered through the laundry room and into the kitchen.

Something smelled good. There were covered pots and pans on the stovetop and Charlie was parked on the couch watching CNN.

"Getting home a little late are we?" he asked, without turning to face me.

"That's shouldn't come as a surprise to you," I said. "I work late all the time."

"My apologies. I assumed you were with Stuart."

I rolled my eyes. "Not tonight. So where'd you order all this lovely food from?"

He thought that was humorous and finally joined me in the kitchen.

"Order? I cook you a full course meal and you insult me by saying I ordered it?"

"Well come on now Charlie, we both know that you in the kitchen is like a fat person at a Tofu convention." We both laughed.

"So silly. But I'll have you know that I cooked all this by myself." He directed me towards the trash so I could see that he made nearly everything from scratch. I was amazed. I've never known Charlie to make toast, let alone cook a full meal.

"You sure you didn't have Sonja come down and cook this?" Sonja was Charlie's maid, cook and personal assistant. She lived in the guest quarters on Charlie's estate—mighty nice I might add. It was a three bedroom, two and a half bath townhouse—altogether, an impressive twenty-two hundred square foot luxury residence.

"Luv, I assure you the only thing Sonja had to do with this meal was emailing me the grocery list for the market." I looked at him, again, even more shocked.

"You? In a supermarket? Charles Thatcher? Get outta here! Now, I *know* you're lying." He handed me his cell phone.

"Go ahead. Call her. She'll tell you." He was trying so hard to convince me.

"You've probably already coerced her into saying you did." I really wanted to believe him. He really wanted me to believe him. I gave in and told him that I believed him, even though I didn't believe him completely. That scenario would have taken all night.

I finished my salad as Charlie set the table with the meal he had created, or *paid* someone to create. It was lobster, four-cheese ravioli in lobster sauce, asparagus, arugula salad and fresh made bread. I would surrender and believe he made everything else tonight before I'd believe he'd made that bread. There was no way. I knew if Stuart knew I was drinking, he'd killing me—so I wouldn't tell him.

After we had our main course, Charlie retrieved chocolate cheesecake from the fridge. I sipped on my wine. It was rather tasty.

"This is good Charlie. What is this?" I asked.

"That's a Cabernet Sauvignon from Judd's Hill in Napa Valley."

"It's very good. How much did a bottle of this set you back, because I know you don't drink cheap wine?" I wasn't prepared for his answer.

"I buy it by the case and a case will put you back about a grand," he said.

I chocked. "Eighty bucks for a bottle of wine?" He nodded. I was flabbergasted.

"If I was *rich*, I wouldn't pay eighty bucks for a bottle of wine."

"But you'd pay seventy bucks for a bottle of Moet?"

"Touché' Mr. Thatcher. Touché." We shared another laugh.

"And you *are* rich, you just don't know it yet," he teased.

"So where are you hiding my lottery ticket?" We shared another laugh. I figured now was as good a time as any to talk to him about Stuart and me. I motioned for him to sit down.

"I knew it was coming sooner than later," he said.

"I want you to be happy for me. I'd be happy for you, if you found the love of your life." *Ouch*. Wrong choice of words.

"I am happy for you Luv. I want to make sure *you're* happy."

"I am. Very much so."

"Well then it's settled," with that he handed me the key to my house. I didn't take it.

"I'm not going to ask for my key back. I need you to keep it just in case. I just want you to be mindful . . . you know . . . when you come over . . . maybe you could call first." I didn't know how to say it without hurting his feelings. To my surprise, he took it like a champ.

He held his hands up. "Hey, I understand. You two need your privacy and I can respect that. But remember what I told you before. If he hurts you, he'll have to answer to me." I smiled at him. Always the protector.

"If he hurts me, I'll hold him down for you. How does that sound?" He smiled at me and placed his hand on top of mine.

"Now that we have that out of the way, are you and my god child ready for cheesecake?"

"You know I love cheesecake. You'd better hurry up!" We enjoyed a couple of more hours together before I left him asleep on the couch. I went upstairs, shut my door and dialed Stuart's number.

We talked for a few moments. Before I knew it, I was awakened by a woman saying, *"If you'd like to make a call, please hang up and try your call again. This is a recording."* I don't know who fell asleep first, but I hung up the phone, turned over in my bed, and went back to sleep.

Chapter 8

I jumped when the phone rang, waking from another sleepless night. I looked at the LCD display on the clock. It was 3.52 a.m. I lifted the receiver to my ear.

"Hello."

"Renee?" said the voice on the other end of the receiver.

"Who is this?" I asked in my usual morning groggy tone.

"It's Susan. You need to call the hospital," she said before I could interject and let her know of my irritation for calling at such an ungodly hour.

"What's going on Susan?" I was alert by this time. I hadn't heard from Susan since the wedding. I knew that for her to be calling as this hour, something serious had to be brewing.

Susan was the open link between my family and me. Even though I was estranged from the majority of my family, Susan kept me up to date on who was doing what, who lost this, and who bought that, who was married and who was divorced—you know, family gossip. On occasion, I talked to my half brother Eddie, but that wasn't often. He hopped from bed to bed so often, he didn't have time to talk to his big sister.

"Just call the hospital," she said. I hung up the phone and dialed the number to St. Joseph's hospital where my mother always stayed.

By this time, Stuart was awake and sat up in the bed at attention. "What's wrong Baby?" he asked.

"I don't know yet," I answered him. "Barbara Jackson's room," I told the operator. The phone rang three times before my mother answered the phone. Stuart held me in his lap, knowing I was about to receive some bad news.

"Hello," she answered weakly.

"Mom, it's me. What's going on?" I asked. I had shocked myself. I called her Mom.

"They foun' a lump on my brain."

I broke loose from Stuart's embrace and stood up on the side of the bed.

"What do you mean they found a lump on your brain?" I asked not understanding. I started pacing the room. "What what are you talking about?"

"A lump," she responded snidely. Stuart was sitting on the side of the bed now right in front of me. I looked at him with terror on my face. He grabbed my hand and sat me back on his lap.

"What happened?" I asked trying to disregard her last comment.

"I had a headache, but dis' time it was worst than the othas." I listened. "My head wudn't stop throbbin', so they took a cat scan and when they ain't find nothin', they took a MRI. Thas' when they found the lump."

"Do they know what it is *exactly*, or what caused it?"

"They don't know yet. They said it coulda been caused by a bump on my head."

I continued to listen attentively, digging deeper into Stuart's sanction. "Have you fallen lately or something?" I asked her.

"No. Only thang I can rememba is when that Mex'can hit my car foe months ago."

"You were in an accident?" I asked nervously.

"Yeah. I ain't thank it was that bad. He hit the right side of my car. My head hit the steerin' wheel real hard, but the docta said I was fine after that."

"Well, how are you feeling now?" I asked, trying to change the monotony. I removed myself from Stuart's lap once more, sat on the window seat and looked out toward the ocean. Nothing but endless darkness—but I knew it was there. Stuart was determined not to leave me alone, so he followed me and sat behind me.

"I'm doin' okay," Barbara Jean said, her tone solemn.

"Who is that I hear in the background?"

"Eddie an' his new gullfrien'. Oh an' Karen."

"Oh," I said. I didn't care too much care for Karen. She was my mother's aunt, had a crooked eye, a gold tooth and was a bitter old bitty.

"Let me speak to Eddie," I finally said. "And I will talk to you tomorrow. I love you." That came from nowhere. I don't know why, but it did—maybe to make her feel comfortable. I honestly don't know.

My brother took the receiver, "Sup," he said.

"How's she really doing?" I asked hm.

"She doin' a'ight. How you doin'?"

"A little worried."

"Yeah, me too."

I listened as my brother gave me the blow by blow on what had happened on his end and what the doctors had told him. I knew my mother wasn't going to tell me everything, and I didn't expect her to. I'm sure she was in no position to think clearly and I didn't want to aggravate her situation.

"Well, I had better get some sleep. I need to make arrangements to get there. I should be there some time . . . " I looked at Stuart for confirmation. He mouthed *tomorrow*. "Tomorrow," I said.

"Okay, talk to you later baby girl."

I replaced the phone on its cradle and stared out towards the ocean once more. Besides a few lights from far away house boats, I could see nothing. Stuart communicated with me, without words. He put his arms around my waist, pulled me close to him and kissed the top of my forehead. We sat there for a while, saying nothing at all. I fell asleep in his arms.

When I woke up later that morning, Stuart was playing in my hair. I looked up to his smiling face. Even though I wore a weave, I had long gotten past being bashful around him.

"Alright, something's going to jump out and bite you," I teased. He just smiled. I couldn't help but notice his eyes were bloodshot red. "What's wrong?" I asked him. Still without words, he handed me a piece of paper where he had written:

Susan cell number 303-555-2715.

My heart felt as if it had sunk into the pit of my stomach. Knowing I was worried, Stuart must have talked to Susan and felt it wasn't important enough to wake me or he didn't want to see me upset.

For a moment, I had to wonder how Stuart felt through all this. We were so happy to have Barbara Jean out of our lives and now, *this*. Although I had disowned her and although Stuart and I had found our way back to each other, I just couldn't abandon her. This time I kissed him on his forehead and I dialed Susan's number.

"Hello?" she answered.

"Hey, it's Renee."

"Have you called the hospital yet?"

"I called last night. Why? Did her results come back?"

"Yes, and they aren't good."

"What's that supposed to mean?" I asked her. Stuart had turned his back away from me. I walked around to his side of the bed and looked at him. He pulled on his jeans and disappeared down the staircase. I understood he was not feeling this.

He had asked me the night before, why after all Barbara Jean had done, would I even consider being there for her.

"Because she's my mother," I told him. Truth be told, her being my mother was far from the truth. It was more guilt than anything. I didn't want to have to answer to God as to why I turned my back on my birth giver during her darkest hour.

"Just call the hospital," Susan said. "And If I were you, I'd go ahead and plan on moving down here."

"What?" I asked. Surely, she didn't just insinuate what I think she did. "I'm not moving down there," I said rebelliously.

"Well I think you should because your mother needs you."

"I'll be there tomorrow, but I'm certainly not moving back to Denver. You're crazy."

"She needs you," Susan pleaded.

"Well she's got another child, nine brothers and sisters and a mother and a host of other relatives there. I'm sure she'll manage just fine."

"I'm not going to argue with you Renee," she said.

"Good. Now let me go so I can call the hospital." I hung up. I called my mother nervous and shaking.

"Hello," Barbara Jean answered in a cheerier voice than she had the day before.

"How are you feeling?" I asked.

"I'm doin' a'ight," she said.

"What did the doctors say?"

"They say I got the canca'."

I wasn't prepared at all for her answer. But it finally sank in. "No Mama!" I shouted as sharp pains took turns jabbing at my chest. I found it hard to breath. Then suddenly I couldn't control the tears, as I fell to the floor in pain. Maybe I was more upset than she was. Stuart had made his way back into the bedroom and caught me as I collapsed onto the floor.

"I'm on my way," I told her before letting the receiver fall to the floor. Stuart hung up the phone, picked me up, and carried me to the bed. He held me for a long time afterwards as I cried, prayed and wondered had I done something wrong.

A sudden change in emotion sent me into denial. I went to my closet and took out a business suit.

"What are you doing?" Stuart asked me.

"Going to work. What do you think silly?"

He looked at me dumbfounded. "I don't think so," he said. "You're going to get ready so we can head to Denver."

"Umm no. I'm going to work. I don't want to hear another word about it," I told him.

I went to take a shower. Reality set back in as I kneeled to the bottom of the shower stall and sobbed uncontrollably. Stuart didn't come to my rescue this time. I think he knew that I wanted to be completely alone right now. If I knew him any better, I was sure he had already arranged for us to fly to Denver—*our* arrangements. There was no way he was going to let me go alone. I didn't want to go alone. However, I knew that bringing Stuart along meant the start of more drama.

After showering and getting dressed, I went into the hallway and looked over the staircase. Stuart was sitting on the sofa staring at the front door. He was now wearing jeans and his signature black t-shirt. He wasn't alone. He had called Charlie. For someone who didn't want Charlie in our relationship, he sure confided in him a lot.

I could see three pieces of luggage by the front door and the silhouette of a limo parked in front of the house. I made my way down the staircase, extended my hand to Charlie and allowed him to kiss it.

"Chuck," I said looking between him and Stuart. "What are you doing here?"

"Just wanted to make sure you're okay."

"I'm fine," I assured him. "Don't tell me you're coming too?"

"Not just yet. I will be there, but I have a meeting with fund directors. After that, I'll be on a plane to Denver."

"You really don't have to," I interjected.

"I wasn't asking you Renee, I was telling you."

I put my hands on my hips and swung my neck around to Stuart.

"You heard the man. You're pregnant. I don't think you should be going anyway, but we know once you have it in your head to do something, you're going to do it. However, I have to make sure you and our baby are safe. And I have to side with Charlie on this one."

I looked at both of them and sucked my teeth as I walked into the kitchen.

My cell phone rang. "Hello."

"Ms. Matthews?"

"Yes?"

"This is Dr. Abrams. Have you arrived here in Denver yet? We are going to operate on your mother pretty quickly."

"When?" I asked.

"Well, as soon as we can get the proper paperwork cleared and get her prepped for surgery. The cancer looks like it has spread."

I asked the doctor how the cancer could have spread so quickly and inquired as to the cause of the cancer.

"It appears that she's had it for a while, but it's hard to say how long. We won't know anything until we are able to operate." I listened without interruption. "I just want to prepare you and your brother for the possibilities," he continued

"And what *are* the possibilities?"

"If we don't operate right away, she *could* die. She could die shortly after the operation. She could live to be one hundred years old. We just don't know, that is why we have to go in," he said, finally pausing for air.

I thanked Dr. Abrams and told him that I would be arriving in a few hours.

"What did the doctor say?" Charlie asked me.

"They don't really know much of anything. They have to operate first."

"When are they going to operate?"

"Today, as soon as they can prep her. I let him know we'd be there in a few hours. Hopefully we'll make it in time."

A few minutes later, my phone rang again. This time it was Susan.

"Renee, the doctor just called us into another family meeting," she said. "They received more test results. She has a Glioblastoma and it's not curable."

"What do you mean it's not curable? They can just go in and remove it right?" I didn't like my aunt's tone. "I just got off the phone with the doctor."

"He just called us in. The cancer has spread across her brain. They are going to operate on her at four o'clock."

"Our plane is supposed to land at two forty five."

"Our?" she asked.

"Yes. *Stuart* and I."

"Oh. Not that he's any better. I thought you were bringing that white man with you. Neither one of them are a part of the family."

"Most of the time I wished I wasn't either," I said and hung up. Certainly, there couldn't be any worse news. I broke down, cried again, and fell into Stuart's arms.

"We'll get through this together," was all he said, holding me. I guess there wasn't much he could say.

On the way to the airport, I wondered what my mother could be going through at this time. I knew she had to be scared and here I was so worried about how I was going to deal with this—with little acknowledgment of her feelings. Before we got to our gate, I called her room.

"Yeah?" It was Eddie.

"Eddie, its Renee."

"Sup bighead? You talk to Mama lately?" he asked me.

"Earlier today when I talked to you. Why?"

"She tell you what the doctor said?"

"That she had cancer?"

"That all she told you?"

"Stop beating around the damn bush," I told him becoming very goaded.

"They say they don't expect her to make it through the surgery."

"Dr. Abrams told me they weren't sure. He said they wouldn't be sure until after the surgery."

"He was in here earlier and called a family meeting, and said the likelihood of her making it through is a million to one. And if she do make it through, they said she won't live that long afterwards."

I let out a deep sigh. "Where is she?"

"Talkin' to Memah and 'nem."

"Let me talk to her for a minute."

"I love you," I told her when she answered the phone. "I'm on my way." I hung up the phone and turned it off. Stuart and I boarded the plane.

I found myself not being able to concentrate. I had no words for Stuart and he had none for me. I nestled my head on his shoulder and tried to read my copy of Barbara Kingsolver's, *The Poisonwood Bible*. I couldn't get into it. I tried writing in my journal. When that didn't work, I asked the flight attendant for a glass of Zinfandel.

Stuart started to interject, but I needed that glass of wine to relax. The baby was just going to have to a bit tipsy for a while.

While I waited for my glass of wine, I thought about how my life was changing drastically right before my eyes. I had struggled for over thirty years to free myself from Barbara Jean Jackson and once I achieved it, here I was, faced with dealing with her once more. Even so, she was still my mother and despite all the things she had done to me, I felt I was doing the right thing.

Once more, I put my life on hold for my mother. Tears rolled down my face as I wondered if I was ready to do this. I had no choice. Stuart and I had reconciled and were going to plan a wedding as soon as we had time.

Ah. Stuart. He too, had to relive this entire saga. I had suggested that he stay in San Diego and let Charlie escort me, but he was not having it.

The flight attendant had returned with my wine. I drank it and as I began to wind down, I started to reminisce on my childhood. I tried to recollect just a few good times, but I found it difficult as I drifted off to sleep.

I drifted.

Back to a time . . . A time I never wanted to go back to again . . .

"Memah, he's coming back. He said when he comes back, he's gonna whip us again."

"I'mma call tha police," Memah said. Barbara Jean and her boyfriend Hal had come home from work the day before and beat my brother and I within an inch of our lives. Earlier that day my brother and I, home alone, snuck into my mother's room to watch television. It was beyond me why I sat a cup of sugar water on top of the television of all the places. Before I could grab it, the sticky liquid had rolled down the back of the television. Eddie and I prayed that it hadn't caused any damage.

We cleaned all that we could and waited to see what would become of the big, bulky nineteen-inch tube. After a few moments, the picture shone as bright as ever, but there was no sound. My brother and I tried everything we could to get the sound to come back, but had no luck.

Later, when Barbara Jean and Hal returned home, they called us into their room.

"Yall bring yall's asses in hea," my mother said. We walked into her bedroom and Hal was trying to fix the television.

"What I tell yall 'bout comin' in my room?"

My brother and I looked at each other and in unison denied that we had been in her room.

"What's wrong with the TV?" Hal asked.

"I dunno," we said in unison shrugging our shoulders. My mother hated when we said *I dunno*. She used to always say she had three kids, Renee, Eddie and I Dunno.

She slapped me. Eddie rarely got the brunt of the punishment.

"I dunno don't live hea. So what tha hell happened to tha TV?" We shrugged our shoulders. She slapped me again. My brother stood at my side as my mother took the brunt of her frustrations out on me.

"What's this sticky shit on the TV," Hal asked. We knew no matter what we did or said we were going to get a whipping. For some reason, however, we thought that if we lied about it, it would soften our blow. We were wrong.

My mother grabbed a nearby extension cord, her discipline of choice, and started swinging at us both. She didn't care where the blows landed as long as they made contact. The more she hit, the angrier she got and when she wasn't satisfied, she turned the extension cord so that the plug was hitting us instead.

That day my mother beat my brother and me within an inch of our lives. To make matters worse, later that night, Hal came in our room while we were sleeping and whipped us out of bed. My mother finally had to stop him. The bruises that we had sustained were so bad, she knew she had to do something or someone was going to start asking questions.

She made us sit in a bathtub full of cold water. She said it made the welts go down. That may have been true, but it had done nothing for the bruises and the welts that seeped blood, and it had done nothing for the pain in my heart.

After my mother and Hal went to work the next morning, I called Memah and told her what had happened.

My grandmother called the police and they were there within minutes. We didn't have the key to unlock the deadbolt so we had to crawl through the living room window.

Chapter 9

I was awakened from my slumber as the captain announced our landing over the overhead system.

"Baby," Stuart said nudging me. "We're about to land."

"You let me sleep the entire trip?"

"You needed it."

After we landed, Stuart and I made our way to a limo that awaited us curbside. When we got to it, the driver was already loading our luggage.

"What time is it?" I asked Stuart.

"Three forty-five," he responded. He seemed a little short. I didn't bother asking him what his problem was, so I ignored him and turned my cell phone's power on. This was just as hard for me as it was for him, if not harder.

Everything looked just as it did when I last saw it, with the exception of a few new buildings. I wondered where I would be had I stayed in Colorado.

My phone rang. Susan.

"Are you here yet?" she asked.

"Yes. We are on our way to the hospital now."

"I'll tell everyone that *you* are on your way."

"You can tell everyone *we* are on our way. Our limo should be pulling up in about ten minutes."

"Oh *we* got a limo huh? To come to a hospital?"

I wasn't about to get into it with her and I certainly wasn't about to explain my accommodations with her.

"Who's at the hospital?" I asked her.

"Everybody, *except* Eddie."

"Nobody has been able to find him yet?" I asked.

"No," she said. I was so mad at my brother. I knew he was off chasing skirts or smoking weed somewhere.

I ventured back to the time when Barbara Jean and I had gotten word that a deranged gang member found Eddie with his girlfriend and killed him. The police said that someone drove by and threw a bomb in the house they were supposed to be in and they had to wait to identify the bodies. They said that the bodies were that of a female and a male fitting my brother's description.

Soon after, the Denver Police Department confirmed, through my brother's dental records, that he was indeed one of the people who died that night.

It wasn't until a few months later that we found out he was still alive. Barbara Jean and I were listening to the radio one night while polishing her brass knick-knacks. Someone called into the station to make a song request.

"What's Up? I want to dedicate *We Are Family* to my mother and my sister so they can stop trippin'."

"Mama that's Eddie!" I said. I knew it was him.

"No it ain't," she rejected. I turned the radio up as we listened. We couldn't believe it. We later found out that he had made a drug run that went bad and had to lay low in Mexico. Not only did he have to worry about whoever wanted him killed, he had to worry about me killing him as soon as I got my hands on him.

Susan had sent me a text to let me know that the doctors could not wait until my arrival before performing the surgery. They had to take Barbara Jean in immediately.

When Stuart and I got to the hospital, I went straight to the cafeteria to buy a bottle of water. Immediately I wished I hadn't come. Several family members were sitting at a large table. They all stopped talking and looked in our direction when they saw us. I didn't acknowledge anyone but my grandmother and my aunt Frieda.

"How are you doing Memah?" I asked my grandmother.

"I'm holdin' on. How you doin'?" she asked.

"As good as to be expected. Memah this is my fiancé Stuart," I said.

"I know who he is," she said. My gut feeling had told me that I had been the subject of conversation before we walked into the cafeteria. My aunt Frieda introduced herself.

"Hi. I'm her aunt Frieda," she said checking Stuart out. She licked her lips as if she was about ready to devour him. I grabbed Stuart's hands and gave aunt Frieda a *you better back off* look. She got the message loud and clear.

"Where is everyone else?" I asked my grandmother.

"In the surgery waitin' room," she said. I got all the information from her and headed towards the elevator bay. Once again, when Stuart and I entered the waiting room, all eyes were on us.

My aunt Susan grabbed my arm and attempted to lead me away from Stuart, as she looked him up and down in disgust. I jerked away from her.

"Don't start no shit," I warned her. I took Stuart by the hand and escorted him to two empty chairs.

Barbara Jean's friend, Anne, was seated by my uncle Lester. The word hate is such a radical word, but I hated my uncle Lester with a passion. Lester was a wife beater and an adulterer. Everyone knew that Lester and Anne had a prior affair, and by the looks of it, they were planning another one. Sad thing about it was that Anne was good friends with Lester's wife.

"Hello Anne," I said pretending that my uncle Lester didn't exist.

"You're looking good Renee." I thanked her. I didn't feel like acting phony right now. It always amazed me how some people could be so bold to think that there weren't consequences to the dirt they played in.

"No one's found Eddie yet?" I asked turning to my aunt Susan.

"He's around here somewhere."

"How long has she been in surgery," I asked referring to Barbara Jean.

"About an hour now," she started. Just then, the doctor emerged from a set of double doors.

"Is Ms. Jackson's daughter here yet?"

"That's me," I held up my finger.

He explained that they were able to remove a good percentage of the tumor. They couldn't remove it all because it would have left Barbara Jean in a vegetative state.

"By taking most of it out and leaving a little in, we're allowing her a better quality of life during the short time she has left.

"What do you mean short time?" I asked. "How long are we talking?"

"Eleven months or so," he answered. Stuart, whom I had forgotten was even there, came up behind me and put his arms around my waist. He wasn't going to let me fall out. Tears streamed from my eyes, but I wanted to keep my composure.

"What is the source of the tumor?" Stuart chimed in. I could hear the sucking of teeth all around.

"Well," the doctor said, as he motioned for us to sit down as he sat next to us. "Glioblastomas are the most aggressive form of cancer as it pertains to the brain. Although, it limits itself to the neurological region, it can cause the tumor to grow, causing swelling in the brain."

"Do we know what causes it?" I asked.

"Well a number of things. Has your mother complained of a fall or any type of head trauma lately?"

"She thought it might have been the car accident she had a couple of months ago." I told the doctor what my mother had told me about her accident. He gave us instruction on how much longer my mother would be in the hospital and arrangements for physical therapy, radiation treatments and chemotherapy.

He explained that he would be moving my mother to the ICU unit for a few days to keep an eye on her. If she improved, she would be moved to a private room.

Everyone around us began to whisper and almost in unison, I heard Susan and Memah gasp. I turned around and realized the subject of their excitement. Charlie had entered the waiting room. I immediately ran to him and gave him a hug, Stuart hot on my tail.

"Are you okay Luv? Is there anything that I can do?"

"No. I'll be okay."

"How are you holding up Stu?"

"I'd rather be a million places than here man, but you know I will support Renee at whatever cost." Charlie nodded his head and patted Stuart on his shoulder. Then the fireworks began.

"Nobody told you to come anyway, you molester and nobody told this white boy to come either," my aunt Susan said.

"You need to mind your own goddamn business," I told her. "And as long as I'm here, my fiancé and best friend will be welcomed here as well. Nobody told you to call me, but you did, so I'm here. So I suggest you sit down and shut the hell up."

"Who the hell you thank you talking to?" my Uncle Lester asked me. I was itching to go rounds with him.

"If I were you, I'd shut the hell up too. Does your wife know where you were last night?" I asked looking from him to Anne. She held her head down. "I didn't think so, so I suggest you leave me the hell alone."

Dr. Abrams broke in on the embarrassing scene, "People. I understand everyone is frustrated about Barbara Jean's condition. But, it will do her no good if she doesn't have a strong support system. She's going to need every single one of you."

He was right, and these people weren't worth me losing my sanity or going to jail—unless *absolutely* necessary. I knew before it was all over with, either Lester or me would be in a hospital . . . or both . . . or jail . . . or dead.

I didn't want Stuart or Charlie ruining their reputation at the hands of my dysfunctional family so I got myself together and received instructions from the doctor and his nurse.

Out of the corner of my eye, I could see my aunt Jasmine looking at me. She had hardly said a word the entire time. I smiled at her and followed the nurse to her station.

I had made plans to spend a great amount of time in Barbara Jean's room. The nurse prepared an expandable chair, next to her hospital bed, for me. I found it a little humorous that everyone wanted to run things, but as soon as I arrived in Denver, they threw everything in my hands. Everyone was ghost.

I tried to convince Stuart and Charlie to go back to the hotel and get some rest, but they would not hear of it. Charlie took his PDA from his jacket pocket and began conducting business, while Stuart chose to read a copy of the Wall Street Journal he bought from the cafeteria.

My aunt Jasmine was still looking at me, all the while saying nothing. I walked over and sat in the chair next to her.

"How are you doing Jasmine?" I asked.

"I'm doing good. How are you?"

"I'm sure you know the answer to that." I slid my feet out of my three-inch slides and rubbed them together for relief.

"How are the children?"

"They're doing good. Bianca starts kindergarten this year and Ashley just got her first tooth." I listened to her as she was more vocal now. Give Jasmine a chance to talk and she'll talk about herself all day long.

I tuned her out for a few moments as I prayed to God to get this whole situation over as soon as possible. I needed Barbara Jean to get better, so I could go home and get back to my life.

"Why don't you all come over to our house for dinner," she said looking me up and down. "You look like you could use a home cooked meal."

I looked at her sideways. It looked as if she had one too many meals. But I realize that since I had been here, she had been the only one to show Stuart, Charlie and I any inkling of kindness.

"What's on the menu?" I asked.

"Fried chicken, ham, fried gizzards, macaroni and cheese, potato salad, yams, greens and banana pudding."

"Good Lord! You sure you're not planning on killing me?" I joked. I had to admit, it had been ages since I had that type of food and I figured one time wouldn't kill me. I would see if I could use my Bally's membership and work it all off.

"I'll ask Stuart and Charlie, but you can count me in." She smiled at me we talked a little while longer about old times.

Chapter 10

Both Stuart and Charlie agreed to go to Jasmine's house for dinner, but they both warned that we would be leaving at the first sign of trouble. I agreed.

Stuart and I went back to our hotel room to rest up before dinner, while Charlie decided to go out and visit some of his Mile High compadres.

We had originally planned on staying at the Holiday Inn at the Airport, but decided to stay at the Embassy Suites closer to the hospital instead.

After we checked in and got to our room, I took off my shoes, turned on the air and plopped down on the bed. I was so tired.

Stuart said something, but I heard none of it, and before I knew it, I was off to sleep, entering a horrifying nightmare.

In my dream, Barbara Jean had died and I was standing over her gravesite plot. I was telling her how much at peace I was since she was gone. I told her all the things I wanted to tell her when she was alive, but didn't because I was too afraid.

In my dream, I was liberated. Just as I was telling her that I would never be like her and I would find love, her hands emerged from the damp soil and grabbed my ankles.

I woke in a cold sweat and called out to Stuart, but he wasn't there. I decided I would take a long hot shower and wash away the dirt and grime of family drama.

I tried to focus on positive things, like finally becoming Mrs. Stuart Humphries. I couldn't wait to start my life as his wife and the mother of his child. I rubbed my belly as I lathered on body wash and smiled. I wondered what my child would be like. What he or she would grow up to be and if they'd make a difference in the world.

When I got out of the shower, Stuart had returned to the room. He had a bag in his hand

"Where'd you go? " I asked.

"To the gift shop to get Tylenol."

"Awww baby, we can cancel dinner and you can just relax."

"No way. I'm actually looking forward to that fried chicken. It's not like I get it back home," he hinted.

I threw a pillow at him. "That stuff will make you fat and then kill you. You saw my family right? If I eat fried chicken, *that's* what you'd have to look forward to."

"You're crazy," he said as he rolled over in laughter. "I can think of a million other things that would kill me." He eased me onto the king sized bed. "Like waiting too much longer to make you *Mrs.* Humphries." He smiled at me with that buttery smile.

Umph, this man is so good to look at.

† † †

The directions Jasmine gave us to her home got us there in no time. Charlie met us there. The house was located in Montbello, a suburb of Denver—the same area my mother lived in. The house was a tri-level cookie cutter.

Jasmine's daughters were the first at the door when we rang the doorbell. Jasmine's husband Obwalla greeted us by shaking our hands and inviting us in. At times, I found it hard to understand him through his thick African accent. Nonetheless, he was a nice man.

The lovely smell of food hit me as soon as we entered. It smelled good, but just as soon as the good smell of food came, it left. It was replaced by a stauncher smell, the closer I got to the living room. I'd recognize that smell anywhere. I smelled it often at Memah's house, especially around the holidays.

Chitlins. Yuck.

"Who'd you cook those cow intestines for?" I asked Jasmine, giving her a hug.

"They're for everybody," she responded.

"Um, I'll pass."

"Still eating white people food," she said before realizing Charlie was in the living room. "Sorry, no offense," she told him.

Charlie smiled at her, "None taken ma'am."

I stayed in the kitchen with Jasmine while Odwalla, Stuart and Charlie talked shop. I found it a wonder that they understood a word he said, but Charlie oversaw the International division at Schwab, so I imagine he had experience with all sorts of thick accents.

Jasmine filled me in on the recent news of her and her family, the girls, and Ashley's fall on her bike. I smiled and listened attentively. I'd always thought Jasmine was so mean that she's never land a man, but she had—even if the rumor was she married him because he offered her a lot of money in exchange for a green card. Who was I to judge? If it worked for them, it worked for me.

I directed my attention to Jasmine and Odwalla's extensive alcohol collection. She followed my gaze.

"You want a drink?" she asked.

"Sure. Something cold and fruity," I said. She showed me where the blender was and gave me all the tools I needed to make a frozen strawberry margarita.

Just as I was turned the blender off, Stuart stuck his head in the doorway."She can't drink." He smiled at me.

I had almost forgotten I was pregnant. How careless of me. "Oopsie," I said. "I nearly forgot."

"You've gotta stop doing that," was his response.

"How far along are you?" Jasmine asked.

"Five months," I responded as I watched Stuart disappear back into the living room.

"Congratulations! I think I want one more. Maybe a boy." She continued talking as she took over where I left off on making that margarita. I guess she figured no use in letting it all go to waste. As we talked, Jasmine had managed to drink two margaritas, a wine cooler and a Jack and Coke.

"Don't you think you should slow down?" I asked her.

"Girl, I'll be fine," she said a little discombobulated.

"Odwalla," I called out teasingly.

"Just as long as she is not driving," he said with that thick accent.

I knew that alcohol and our family did not mix. Hell, I knew that alcohol, black folk and good food did not mix.

Jasmine and I set the table in the dining room and summoned the men folk to join us. She asked Stuart to say grace and he obliged.

After grace, everyone dug into the feast before us. I couldn't wait to get my hands on that fried chicken and boy was it good. The yams with brown sugar and marshmallows were a welcomed treat.

I was so concentrated on my food that I hadn't heard what Charlie had said. Before I knew it all eyes were on me. I was so embarrassed. I looked up and scanned everyone around the table.

"What?" I asked innocently.

"I was telling Jasmine here that we'd have to either fly her to San Francisco or fly Sonja here to Denver so she can learn how to cook this delicious soul food. "

I looked at Charlie, I knew he was just being nice, or was he? I've never knew Charlie to like soul food. Had I known, I would have cooked it for him even though I stayed away from these types of delicacies. I worked hard getting myself in shape and it would be a shame to let it go at this point.

"So Renee, I've been thinking for a while," Jasmine said. I gave her my undivided attention—well of course in between bites of corn bread and greens.

She continued, "Have you ever wondered why only you and I were born in a hospital and everyone else was born at home with the help of a mid-wife?"

I stopped chewing. I was sure the alcohol had her delusional and she didn't know what she was saying, because I sure didn't know what she meant. I humored her.

"What do you mean?"

"Well. You and I are the youngest and are the only two born in a hospital. Doesn't that seem strange to you?"

"Well, truthfully, I never thought about it. But I have to be honest, I didn't know that you and I were the only two that were born in a hospital."

Charlie and Stuart looked at each other then at me as they continued to enjoy their vittles.

"I'm a little confused Jasmine," I told her.

"Hear me out for a second. Think about all of us." I knew all of us included all my aunts and myself. We were practically sisters, even though I had a different last name. I had asked Barbara Jean before why we had a different last name than the rest of the family and she always told me to stop trying to mind grown folks business. When I asked Memah, she told me that back then a black family couldn't get help from the county if they were married, so in order to have Barbara Jean in a hospital, she had to tell them she was a single mother. I believed the story at first, but I wondered why Barbara Jean couldn't be delivered at home via a midwife like everyone else. I never pursued the issue.

"I'm still not following you," I told Jasmine.

"You and I are related," she said.

"Of course we are silly. You're my aunt." I was thinking she really needed to lay off the alcohol as she took another sip of a third margarita. I wasn't prepared for what she said next.

"No, I mean, we have the same mother," she said. I nearly choked on my iced tea.

"What did you say?" I asked her. She repeated what she had said. "I think you've had one too many drinks," I laughed uncomfortably scanning everyone at the table.

"I'm a little tipsy but I'm not drunk. Listen to this, have you ever asked Barbra Jean why she was born at the hospital and everybody else was born at home? Or why we all don't have the same last name?"

"Actually I did ask her that, but she told me to stay in a child's place in so many words. When I asked Memah, she told me some story about having to say that she and Paw weren't married so she could get help and have mom at the hospital." I had to wonder why we were repeating ourselves.

Jasmine looked at me with a blank stare that made me feel even more uncomfortable. "Why would there be a need to have Barbra Jean in a hospital and not at home like everyone else?"

"I don't know. Like I said, I've never really given it much thought after that."

"Let me tell you why. Something wasn't right about Paw." I looked at her, prepared to go on the defensive.

"What do you mean . . . something like *what*?"

"Let's just say Paw didn't know how to keep his hands to himself," she continued. "The first time, he and Rosie thought they could pass me off as her child, but when he continued to *touch* Barbara Jean, they ended up sending her away."

"What the hell are you talking about?" My chest was starting to hurt. Stuart stood up and came around to my chair.

"Do we need to do this now?" he asked.

"Yes!" Jasmine screamed. "I think it's about time she knew. Somebody has to tell her. We can't let Barbara Jean and Rosie take this to their graves. She deserves to know where she came from. Now sit down, shut up and listen!"

Stuart looked at me for confirmation, I nodded and he sat back in his seat. I wasn't prepared to believe her lies, but common sense told me to listen to her. It wasn't the first time that I had heard rumors of foul play in our family.

"Now, Renee, you and I are only two years apart in age. Jessie Lee, I mean Paw molested Barbara Jean repeatedly, but as the years passed, it got worse."

I gasped and held my chest. Charlie lowered his head and I had to wonder why he was being so quiet. Usually, he was so attentive and catering to my every whim, but now, he sat in silence. It was almost as if he knew something I didn't. I allowed Jasmine to continue, but I kept my eyes on Charlie.

"You and I are not the only spawn of Barbara Jean. We were just the ones who made it out of the womb."

"Why are you speaking these lies? If Barbara Jean bore us both, then that means we are sisters."

"Bingo!" she said taking another drink of her liquid courage.

"That's impossible," I refuted. Charlie still refused to look at me.

"Okay, you're not getting it. So let me just say it without all this sugar coating. Paw couldn't keep his hands off Barbara

Jean. For some reason, he didn't mess with the other girls. No, Barbara Jean was different. I still haven't figured that part out. I don't even believe that Barbra Jean was Paw's child. I believe that Rosie, I mean Memah was already pregnant when she met Paw and passed Barbara Jean off as his. "

I could feel sweat form in my scalp, under my tracks and roll down the back of my neck. I drank more ice tea to cool off. All of this great food before me and I had a sudden loss of appetite.

"Should the children be present during this?" Charlie finally spoke. Odwalla agreed and took the girls upstairs to their room and stuck a movie in the VCR.

"Anyway, I was a result of Paw molesting Barbara Jean. Susan told me she overheard Rosie and Jessie Lee talking about how nobody was going to find out about what he had done. She said Paw said he'd promised to never do it again. But then Paw got more violent in his attacks on Barbara Jean. Susan said she thinks it was because Paw knew Barbara Jean wasn't his."

Odwalla had returned to the table and Jasmine acknowledged his presence by asking him if the girls were okay and out of sight. He confirmed that they were all right and assured that they would be entertained for the next hour by the Power Puff Girls.

Stuart looked at me and gave me an *are you okay* look. I nodded. I nodded in Jasmine's direction, allowing her to continue.

"Paw used to beat Barbara Jean so bad, she missed school because of scars, cuts, black eyes, you name it. Memah told him if he didn't stop, she was going to leave him."

"So why didn't she tell anyone?" I asked.

"Girl, you know black folk in the day didn't air their dirty laundry. Incest runs rampant in our family. Hell, every other black family for that matter. We just don't tell folks, like these white folks be all up in the TV, or writing books about their stuff. No offense Charlie." Charlie nodded his head.

"So where do I come in?" I asked.

"Well, Memah never did make good on her promise to leave Paw, so he continued doing what he was doing. After a while, Memah would just let him. It was like she fed Barbara Jean to the wolves. She would leave the house to go to the store or to church and take all kids with her, except Barbara Jean."

Although this all seemed a bit absurd, it wasn't all that farfetched. I paid attention to the whispers at family reunions or comments family members would make when they would come into town. When I was younger and staying with Memah, I overheard a few conversations that I probably shouldn't have heard. However, I was young and had no intelligence to question her.

"I remember this day as clear as I know my name. I overheard Susan telling Beatrice, about Memah taking them all to church one Sunday." Beatrice was another one of my aunts. "Well, all of them except for Barbara Jean. They asked why Barbara Jean got to stay home when they had to go to boring old church. She told them that Barbara Jean stayed in trouble and had to be left behind to do the chores.

"Well, when they got home from church, Paw Paw and Barbara Jean was in the backyard by the washing barrel. Barbara Jean was slumped over it and Paw Paw was standing over her. When he turned around, Barbara Jean's body fell to the ground. They thought she was dead. She took a deep breath and tried to hold back tears.

"Do you want to stop now?" Odwalla asked her, giving her a glass of ice water. She declined to stop, but gladly took the ice-cold water.

"Paw ran to get the doctor and when he got back I specifically remember Memah asking him how Barbara Jean got that knot on her head. I mean the knot was so big, it looked like a baseball. But Susan said Memah already knew what happened. It had been happening for a long time and this time Paw had taken it too far.

"Well, when the doctor checked Barbara Jean out, he told them that she had been raped. She had a lot of damage done to her uterus and she had two broken ribs."

I gasped and stopped her for a moment. "Jasmine, why are you telling me this? Why are you telling me all this *now*?"

"Because Barbara Jean may not make it. You need to know why she's loopy like she is. You need to know why it's possible you haven't gotten past some of your issues and you need to know for your children's sake."

That made sense to me and what made even more sense were Barbara Jean's actions. If this was all true, it would explain why she always acted as if she was jealous of me, or why she wanted to see me suffer. She *was* bitter, and she wanted me to suffer like she did.

"The doctor, I forget his name, but he also told them that Barbara Jean was pregnant. The day that the doctor came to the house, we were in our room, but the older kids heard him when he told them. The doctor asked them if they knew who could have done this. They both said no, but I knew that the doctor knew better. The doctor also told them that because of the damage to Barbara Jean's uterus, he didn't think it was a good idea to attempt to have the baby. Well, let's just say, the very next day, Barbara Jean was on a train from Monroe to Colorado Springs."

"So she was already pregnant when she got to Colorado Springs?"

"Yea."

"I asked my mother about my father when I was younger. She tried to pass me off on a soldier she met at Peterson Air Force base. When I asked her why they weren't still together, she told me some bogus story about him lying on the couch one day and she asked him for money for an Easter basket. He threw her a dollar and she in turn threw hot grease on him. She said he left and never came back."

"That was a lie," Jasmine said.

"Well when she found the opportunity to pawn me off on this guy she was talking about, I accepted him as my father. His name was Donald McKnight. I went to stay with him and his family. When I asked him why he left Barbara Jean, he told me they were never together. He said he met her at the NCO club on the base and they had a one-night stand and that was the end of that. He said she showed up years later stating I was his."

I stopped for a moment and thought back. Donald had told me that he and his family—his wife and kids, lived on the next block. He said he and Barbara Jean never had a relationship. He said that after their one-night stand, he hadn't heard from her until I was nearly a teenager.

I can remember the scenario when I first met him. The funny thing is that I had seen this man several times before. Memah, Barbara Jean, and me, would frequent the infamous flea market in Commerce City. He and his wife were vendors and I bought their earrings all the time. The sad thing is, although I hadn't a clue who he was, he knew *exactly* who *I* was. Finally, one day, Memah got fed up.

"Renee, this is your father, Donald," she introduced us. I looked at him and then to Barbara Jean, who I'm sure wished she could be anywhere but there. I looked back to the stranger, said hello, and walked off. I mean, what did they expect me to do? How did they expect me to react? I was fourteen-years-old, and all this time, this man knew I was his child but never bothered to let me know. It made sense to me though. His wife was white and he had no room for a "blackie" in his family tree. At least, that was how I felt on that very day—and what Barbara Jean told me later.

Donald and his wife had three other children, also white, and as if it wasn't bad enough that Barbara Jean made me feel inadequate, this Donald guy put the nail in the coffin.

"I can't believe she let me believe he was my father. I can't believe she let him believe he was my father," I said out loud, more to myself than anyone else.

"I gather it was easier for her to say you were the result of a failed relationship rather than an act of rape. Funny . . . Life."

I saw nothing funny about it at all. Most of my childhood, I wondered why the white doll was better than the black doll. I wondered why whites were treated better than blacks and I wondered why after the pain and scars of slavery, why black men found white women more attractive than black women. I was so messed up. I began to realize as I got older that those were myths and that because black families hide their dirt and take away the opportunity to heal, they really screwed our race—especially our women.

"So why was I blacklisted and you weren't?" I asked Jasmine.

"I really can't answer that Renee. But I gather since it happened so long ago and Memah actually raised me as her own, and because Paw promised he'd never do it again, I became one of them."

"Have you ever confronted Barbara Jean about this?"

"Of course I have. On several occasions. Each time she'd tell me I was trying to start trouble and it'd end there. But I made sure that she knew that *I* knew the truth and I made sure she knew that if she or Memah didn't tell you, *someone* would. I guess she figured with all the other molestation and incest issues in this family, she was off the hook because it took the attention off her."

I didn't know how to rap my head around what I had just learned. Part of me did not want to believe Jasmine, but I had to use common sense. I finally turned my attention to Charlie who was now beet red.

"You've been awfully silent *and* still Charlie," I said *very* dryly. I knew he knew something. Right after Barbara Jean interrupted my wedding, he had put a call out to find information on both Stuart and Barbara Jean, but he never gave me the results of that so-called investigation.

"I know you know something. Out with it."

"Luv, I really don't think . . ."

"Charlie! Don't you dare patronize me."

"I don't know everything in depth, but I did verify the basics of what your aunt has revealed here today. I knew who your real father was and I knew about the cover up . . ."

"What? How *long* have you known?" I yelled.

"A few months," he revealed.

"A few months?

I was furious. I stood from the table. "A few months? A few months Charlie? You mean to tell me that after all this time you've known and you allowed me to enter the lion's den and didn't tell me?" I poured the rest of what was left of my iced tea in Charlie's face.

"Stuart I need to leave." Stuart was already by my side. He knew for sure I was going to kill Charlie. He held both my arms.

He turned to Jasmine. "Jasmine, thank you for the food and the hospitality, and although I felt that you could have chosen better circumstances to tell my fiancé, I'm somewhat relieved that you did. I just wished she wasn't pregnant. She doesn't need to be under this kind of stress."

Jasmine stood up. "I cannot apologize for telling her what I thought she should know, but I didn't mean to cause her any stress. But, when *is* a good time to tell someone something like this? I felt it was best she knew before Barbara Jean passed." She wiped her tear stained face with her napkin as Odwalla came to her aid.

I gave her a hug. "Thank you for being the one to be *honest* with me about this. And thank you for telling me. If it wasn't for you, I don't know if I would have ever found out. It explains a lot." I looked at Charlie in fury. I wanted to throw more than my tea at him. I sucked my teeth and Stuart escorted me to our car.

Chapter 11

I laid my head back on the headrest of our rental car. I had asked Stuart to rent one just so I didn't have to hear my family's comments about having a service car. He settled on a Chevy Suburban. He turned to me and smiled. He didn't speak at first. I knew he was trying to feel me out and decide if he should say anything. I gave him his opening.

"What?" I asked.

"You know I love you, but that was wrong what you did back there?"

"*No*, what was wrong was Charlie keeping that from me. He should have told me. He had no right to do that." I was angry, and the more I thought about it, the angrier I became.

"Renee, since I've known you and Charlie, he has always had your best interest at heart. He wouldn't do anything to purposely hurt you."

"Look, this is another way for Charlie to control me—something he's done since I've known him."

"Whose fault is that though?"

I looked at him defensively "What is that supposed to mean"

"Baby, think about it. Charlie has been protective of you since day one. I've heard you say several times that it bothers you sometimes, and then other at times, you've used it to your advantage."

I crossed my arms across my chest. I knew he was right, but I wasn't going to admit it. Besides, that wasn't the point.

Charlie had valuable information that would affect my life, and he kept it from me.

"I'm sure you had to know *something* about what Charlie was doing. I can't imagine Charlie doing anything without letting you know."

He was right, I was there when Charlie ordered the background check on both he and Barbara Jean. "The bottom line is he kept it from me. That was *not* the place for me to find out."

"That may be true, but I think pouring the drink on Charlie was a little dramatic and unnecessary."

"Whose side are you on?"

"This is not about sides, this is about what's right. And that, my dear, was not right."

I knew he was right. Charlie had been there for me from the start and had always been my protector. I still think he should have told me *when* he found out, but I did owe him an apology. It looked like we both owed the other a little forgiveness.

I reclined my seat and laid back. We rode to the hotel in silence. I replayed the night's events in my head. I would apologize to Charlie . . . *later*. The more pressing issue was the information had I learned tonight. My aunt Jasmine was always a little suspect, but deep down inside, I knew by the look on Charlie's face there had to be a little truth to what she had told me.

Actually, it explained a lot. It explained why Barbara Jean, Eddie and I were the black sheep of the family. It also would explain why Barbara Jean despised me so much. The thought of it all tired me out. I dozed off and was awakened when Stuart gently shook my arm.

When we got into our hotel room, I collapsed on the bed. Stuart removed my shoes and massaged my feet. It felt so good that I fell into a deep sleep.

Drifting . . .

Drifting . . .

Drifting . . .

"Mom, I've always wondered this, but I never knew how to ask you," I said to Barbara Jean one day while I was helping her hang a picture. She looked at me and rolled her eyes, but didn't give me an answer. I wanted to know, no, I *needed* to know.

"I'm serious. I think I have the right to know why I have a different name, why *you* have a different name than the rest of the family."

"Why you tryna' be in somebody's business? That ain't got nothin' to do wit' you?"

"What do you mean it has nothing to do with me? It has *everything* to do with me."

"I'm not talkin' 'bout dis' to you and don't ast me again." Ast, not ask.

I don't know why I never asked Memah the reason. It could have been because I stopped asking questions after I had asked her why she treated us so badly.

Her response, "I did the best I could considerin'."

"Considering? Considering what?"

"Considerin' the circumstances, and thas all you need ta' know. Stop askin' questions."

I would leave it alone, but I had one more question.

"Why does mama hate me so much?" I asked her.

"'Cause yo' mama ain't right. She fell out a car when she was little and she ain't been right since. All huh hair fell out too."

So, my mother had a head injury and it wasn't *her* fault that she treated me so bad. I was content with that explanation and didn't ask again.

† † †

I woke up early the next morning, still in the clothes from the night before. Stuart was sitting in the sitting area reading the morning paper, drinking coffee and eating fruit.

"Good morning," I said, walking up behind him and massaging his shoulders. He ran his hand over mine.

"Good morning sleepy head. How do you feel? You were out like a light."

"I had no idea I was so tired.'

"Considering last night's events, it's totally understandable."

I kissed him on the top of his head and ate the strawberry from his hand.

"I thought you were allergic to strawberries."

"I am. I'll pay for it later, but I'm famished."

Stuart chuckled.

"What's so funny?" I asked him.

"Famished. You've been around Charlie too much."

I rolled my eyes at him and sat on the sofa. "Speaking of Charlie I need to call and apologize.'

"Would you like me give you some privacy?" Stuart asked me.

"Please," I answered.

Stuart kissed me on the forehead and told me he was going to take his laptop to the lobby and check his email.

Once he was gone, I dialed Charlie's number. He answered after the third ring.

"Good morning Luv."

"Good morning Charlie. Are you still in Denver?"

"Where else would I be?"

"I was sure that after last night's debacle, you'd be back in San Francisco by now."

"I don't know what made you think that. I came here to support you. That hasn't changed."

"Look Charlie, I'm sorry about last night. I thought you'd be the last person to hurt me, but after I cooled down, I realized you were just trying to protect me. I'm sorry I acted such a fool last night. I just wish you had told me."

"I know Luv, but I didn't know how to tell you. I certainly didn't expect it to come about like *that* and actually, I was hoping that your mother would tell you herself."

Charlie was right, it should have come from my mother *or* Memah. Now that I knew, I wasn't quite sure what I'd do with that information. In the meantime, I had a lot to make up to Charlie.

"Do you forgive me for being such a witch?" I asked him.

"There's nothing to forgive. I can't even imagine how I'd react, if I found out what you found out last night and in the manner in which you found out. All is forgiven and forgotten. Just remember this Renee, it's going to take a lot more than a glass of iced tea to the face to stop me from loving you. And, might I add that at least it was good iced tea. Your aunt Jasmine is one hell of a cook." We both chuckled.

Charlie knew me well and had a way of making me laugh. That was priceless and I never wanted to lose that.

"Do you forgive me for waiting to tell you?" he interrupted my thoughts.

"Nothing to forgive, right?" I used his sentiments against him.

"Right! Now let's change the subject. What's on the agenda for today?"

"Well, they're moving Barbara Jean to a regular room today, so I need to go to the hospital to make sure *that* runs smoothly and then make sure she has plenty to eat."

"Do you need me to be there?"

"No, Stuart and I will be alright. However, Stuart has to go into the Cherry Creek office for a teleconference around lunchtime. Do you want to take your old friend to lunch?"

"I thought you'd never ask. I'll pick you up around, let's say, twelve-thirty? That way Stuart can drive to the office and won't have to worry about dropping you off."

"Sounds good to me. Love you Charlie," I said.

"Love you too Luv," he responded before hanging up the phone.

I jumped in the shower and turned the water on as hot as I could bear. I needed to wash the remnants of last night off as much as possible. I knew today would be an interesting day. There would be no way that I would *not* mention this to my mother. I was getting closer to the truth of knowing who I was. I wasn't about to stop now.

When I finished my shower, Stuart was back in our hotel room watching MSNBC. He looked exhausted.

"I figured you where in the shower when I called and you didn't answer."

"I'm sorry babe. How are you feeling? You're looking a little tired. You know, you can sleep in and I can go to the hospital by myself. It's no big deal."

Stuart gave me a blank stare and held it for at least thirty seconds.

"What's that all about?" I asked.

"You're crazy if you think that I'm going to let you go there by yourself this morning, after what happened last night. I know you Renee. The first chance you get, you're going to bring it up, and there's a great chance that after that, all hell will break loose. There's no way I'm letting you go by yourself."

"But Stuart," was all I got out before he gave me that *'woman I have spoken now sit down and be quiet'* look. I obeyed.

† † †

An hour or so later, Stuart and I were at the hospital. I checked in at the nurse's station and received instruction from the charge nurse as to the day's activities. Stuart thought he should sweeten the blow of what was to come by stopping by McDonald's to get Barbara Jean bacon, eggs and pancakes.

When we walked into her room in the ICU, she was looking towards the door. When she saw Stuart, she turned away. I rolled my eyes.

"Good morning Barbara Jean," he said to her.

"What tha hell you doin' hea'?" she spewed.

"Supporting my soon to be wife. Now, I know the food here can't be too good, so I, *we*, brought you something from McDonalds."

"I don't want nothin' you got to offa," she said. I was about to interject when Stuart held up his hand.

"You know Barbara Jean, McDonalds charged me six dollars for this breakfast, and I'll be damned if you're not going to eat it. You can hate me all you want, but you're going to eat this food." He sat it on a nearby serving tray, unwrapped it and pulled the tray over her bed. She turned her head away.

"Eat the damn food Barbra Jean," he said, his patience running thin. She looked at him with surprise in her eye.

"Mama, just eat the food. You know you want it. I don't know why, after God has given you another chance, you still insist on being Betty Bad Ass. Not everyone gets a second chance. Just go with it will ya?"

She rolled her eyes at me, looked at Stuart and said, "If you eva talk ta me like that again . . . an' next time, you betta brang mo' butta."

I rolled my eyes again. This woman was impossible, but at least she got the message. I'd wait until she was done with her breakfast before I brought up the past.

One of the duty nurses came in to check on my mother and let us know that someone would be in shortly to move her to her new room. She handed me paperwork and instructions on the care she would receive and the whole bit.

Before I had signed the last piece of paperwork, two orderlies appeared at my mother's door. Stuart and I gathered my mother's belongings and followed them to the elevator and up to what would be my mother's permanent room for weeks to come.

Once she was in her private room, I tried to set up her room to make it look as homey as possible.

"Mother, what would you like for lunch?" I asked. I informed Stuart that while he was away at his teleconference that Charlie and I would be going to lunch.

"Humph. You gone to let huh go with that white man?"

"Mind your business Barbara Jean. If it wasn't for that white man, your daughter wouldn't be here today. I tried to convince her not to even come to Denver. So, just like your daughter, just like me, start showing that white man some respect. If you plan on having any kind of relationship with your daughter, you'd better get used to all three of us."

Barbara Jean looked at Stuart and then to me and asked, "What kinda crazy mess yall got goin' on?"

"It's called love Mama, something you'd never understand. Now drop it. Now, what do you want for lunch woman?"

"You know what I want."

"I should have figured. Do you eat anything besides chicken?"

"You gone buy me some lobsta'?"

"If that's what you want."

"I ain't playin'."

"I'm not either mother. Is that what you want?"

"Can I have chicken fa' lunch and seafood fa' dinna?"

"Yes ma'am. You've got it," Stuart answered for me.

"Mama, I need to ask you something?" I began. It was now or never. The door to her room was becoming a revolving one with numerous medical staff.

She rolled her eyes. "Wheneva' you ask that, you wanna know somethin' that you ain't' got no business askin' 'bout."

"Did Paw rape you? And is he my *real* father?" I blurted out. Stuart turned to face the window. Barbara Jean stopped in mid-chew. I could tell by the look on her face that I had hit a nerve and at that point, I knew it was the right nerve.

"Who tha hell tole you dat?"

"It doesn't matter who told me, is it true?" I got my answer when tears started streaming down her face.

"I tole you long time ago, you need ta stop gettin' in business that ain't got nuthin' to do wit' you."

"What do you mean nothing to do with me? My mother was brutally raped, repeatedly by her father, and I was a result to one of those brutal rapes. What do you mean it has nothing to do with me? Why is this family so damned delusional?"

"Watch yo' mouth and let sleepin' dogs lie."

"Why should I let sleeping dogs die? You've let me walk around all this time believing that Donald was my father, when you've known the truth all this time."

"I ain't wanna relive the past," she said.

"Why do you always think that everything is about you? Just like when your brother raped me. You had the nerve to disown me and then ten years later you tell me you were ready to deal with it. And on top of that, you wanted to take it to Oprah. That wasn't about you, just like this isn't. If you don't want to deal with what Paw did to you, I understand. But keeping from me that I was a result of that rage and wrong doing is just wrong. You should be ashamed of yourself." I was very upset at this point.

Stuart put his hand around my waist and whispered in my ear to chill out. I walked over to window looking for a view, but all I got was another tall building. I would let it go. After all, I had the truth now, and really, what could I do with it? Paw was dead, I was in my thirties, and truth be told, there was absolutely nothing that I could do about it . . . *except* to get counseling.

At about 12:15 p.m., Charlie walked through the door. "I thought it'd take an act of congress trying to find you all," he said. He had a bouquet of roses in his hands and balloons.

"For you, my lady," he said handing them to Barbara Jean. Barbara Jean looked at Charlie in suspicion, then at me. I gave her an evil scowl and mouthed say *thank you*.

"Uh, thank you, I thank," she said.

"Just a little something to brighten your day," Charlie responded.

"Charlie you didn't have to, but I'm glad you did," I said. Charlie smiled at me as he and Stuart exchanged pleasantries.

"I'm heading out babe," he told me and then gave me a kiss on the lips. After he hugged me, he turned to Charlie, "You take care of my Queen now."

"Always Mr. Humphries, always."

"Barbara Jean," Stuart acknowledged my mother and nodded his head. "I'll be back shortly with your two-piece white." With that, he was out the door.

Several nurses and doctors were in and out of my mother's room taking vitals and giving her instructions. Charlie and I decided to get out of the way and head out to lunch.

Chapter 12

"How long you gone sleep? I'm hungry," I heard Barbra Jean say. I had decided to stay the night in her hospital room. Her doctor said that her blood pressure had gone up and had diagnosed her with Diabetes. I was a bit worried, and would have felt bad if something had happened to her and I was not there.

I looked at her, "Payback for when Eddie and I were little and you'd sleep all day and not get up to feed us." I got up, grabbed my toiletry bag and headed into the restroom. I brushed my teeth, and washed my face. I heard Stuart enter the room and greet my mother. I could smell food. Good, now I didn't have to go out and get anything.

"Good morning Barbara Jean. Where's my baby?"

"Stuart," was all I heard her say.

After I combed my hair, I exited the bathroom, wrapped my arms around Stuart and laid my head on his chest.

"You okay babe?" he asked.

"Yes. Just a little tightness in my back."

"I'll give you a massage later. Are you hungry? I brought something from Denny's."

I had stopped eating at Denny's over a year ago after a racism claim was filed against the restaurant when one of the employees was accused of spitting in one of its patron's food. I swore then that I'd never eat at Denny's ever again. I put that in the back of my mind as my stomach growled at the savory smell of bacon, eggs, biscuits and gravy.

"I thought you ain't like Denny's," Barbara Jean said.

"I won't tell if you won't," I responded stuffing bacon in between my chops. She rolled her eyes at me as she stuffed hers.

A few moments later, a nurse came in to check Barbara Jean's vitals. Her blood pressure had come down, but it would surely rise again with all the bacon she was consuming. The nurse advised her that she would be ordering Barbara Jean a low-sodium lunch, and informed her that she would have to lay off fried foods for a while.

"I was hoping for some fried catfish from Pierre's for dinner," she said. She was trying to milk Stuart and I recognized it. We had spent more money on her than we cared to admit. Barbara Jean was always nice as long as you were spending your money on her. I guess part of my guilt obliged in her manipulation but there was only so far I was willing to go.

† † †

Weeks had passed and Barbara Jean was receiving radiation, chemotherapy and physical therapy to help her live the best quality of life she could in her condition. The doctors were quite optimistic saying she was getting stronger as the days went by.

One day, after the doctor had come in to talk to Barbara Jean, I asked him if I could speak to him privately in the hallway.

"So doctor, with her improvements, is there a chance she can shake the cancer?"

"Unfortunately not. Although your mother is getting stronger, she is merely improving the days that she has left. So, instead of having bad days, they will be better days. The cancer is still spreading and her prognosis is still the same. Our diagnosis of eleven months still has not changed."

Eleven months . . . Eleven months . . .

I tried to wrap my head around that. I finally dismissed it. As far as I was concerned, God had the final say so, and no doctor was going to tell me that my mother had exactly eleven months to live. He wasn't God, and he couldn't make that kind of prediction. Barbara Jean had made great strides since the surgery and was back to her old, surly self.

"What was that about?" she asked me when I came back into the room.

"Trying to find out when you can go home," I lied. The look on Stuart's face told me he knew I was fibbing.

I changed the subject. "When was the last time, someone has come to visit you?" It seemed that since I had been there and as the days went by, those who appeared to be concerned about my mother, no longer saw a need to come and visit her. Occasionally someone would drift in to see how she was doing, but visits were few and far between.

"Some folks from the church came by yesterday," she responded.

"What about your family?" I asked.

"Now you just bein' messy," she said.

"I thought it was a valid question."

An orderly knocked on the door before he entered the room and asked if Barbara Jean was ready to go down for physical therapy. I hadn't gone to any of her previous sessions but wanted to go to this one to see how her progress was coming along. Stuart opted to go to the cafeteria and make phone calls.

Barbara Jean seemed to be doing very well in physical therapy. She was walking now, which was a good sign. Her physical therapist worked on trying to get her to use her cane as opposed to depending on her walker. She said she was afraid of falling, and I could understand that.

In addition to being able to walk, her range of motion skills were improving, although occasionally she complained of pain in her head when she had to think too hard. At times, it was hard to watch her. I witnessed the spunky, mean-spirited, designer wearing shell of my mother dissipate.

After her physical therapy sessions, Barbara Jean was transferred to radiology for her chemo and radiation treatments. She was going four days a week and it was taking its toll on her. Usually, after a treatment, she would sleep for the rest of the day.

I was becoming a bit antsy, because the hospital life had worn out its welcome. I was ready to get Barbara Jean out of there and get her home so she could get back to normal, move on with her life and I could go back home to San Diego and *my* life. I missed my house, I missed my job, I missed my city and I missed my comfort zone. There was nothing more that I'd rather be doing at this moment than sitting on a beach, reading a book.

After Barbara Jean fell asleep, I texted Stuart a message.

6195550606:	*What are you up to?*
6195553156:	*Working on a report. You?*
6195550606:	*BJ is sleep. So sick of this hospital.*
6195553156:	*Want to go out for a bit?*
6195550606:	*Please and thank you.*
6195553156:	*Will be up in a min.*

Stuart walked into the door about ten minutes later and Barbara Jean was still sleeping. I left her a note that I was going out for a bit and made sure that the nurse had my number just in case she needed us.

Initially Stuart and I had planned on going to one of the downtown pubs, but I wanted to eat and crash. We opted for room service and the comfort of the hotel bed instead. After eating a good portion of my Thai chicken salad, I showered and lay across the bed.

"Are you ready for that massage I promised you?" Stuart asked.

"Yes sir," I responded.

His hands felt good on me. I realized that it had been a while since I had felt his touch like this or since my man and I had experienced intimacy. After Stuart performed his miracle on me, I performed one on him.

✝ ✝ ✝

A few days later, Dr. Abrams informed us that Barbara Jean would be cleared to go home. I was relieved. He said that she had improved greatly—she was walking on her own and could take care of herself.

He advised us to hire a home health nurse to assist Barbara Jean with her daily activities. Although he was confident that she could take care of herself, he warned that things could change in an instant.

I scheduled doctor's appointments, physical therapy appointments and nursing and health aide visits for Barbara Jean. She would be released from the hospital in a few days, and I wanted to make sure she was comfortable and had everything she needed at home.

"The doctor said you can go home on Saturday," I told Barbara Jean.

"I bet you glad. You gone go back to San Diego?"

"Well, I'll stay with you for a while. You seem to be doing okay, but I *will* be going back home soon."

"This *is* yo' home. What you talkin' bout?"

"No, this is not my home. This is where I was raised. But, I don't feel at home here. San Diego is my home," I said. Barbara Jean rolled her eyes at me. I knew that the old Barbara Jean was about to rear her ugly head.

"So what I'm sposed ta do when you gone?"

"Live," I shrugged. "You have tons a family here. There's no reason you shouldn't be able to get any help." I know I was trying to convince her and myself. It had been a while since anyone from the family had come to the hospital to visit her. When they thought she was dying, they all rallied around her, pretending to care. Of course, then, they thought there would be something in it for them . . . like money. But now that she was improving and it looked like she would make it, she served no purpose to them.

"We both know betta'," was all she said.

"Let's just concentrate on getting you better. You've always been independent. I don't see why this has to be any different. Your speech has improved, you're walking on your own and you never lost your appetite. That alone, should be a healing for your soul. I have no doubt that you'll be able to take care of yourself."

"Humph. Since you brought up food, I'm hungry," she said.

"Charlie is bringing lunch from La Hacienda."

"That white boy still hea'?"

"You need to stop. That's why you're in the predicament you're in now, because you're so evil." I could see my mother's mind spinning. She was looking for a reason to make me mad, in hopes that I'd run off so she could tell everyone that I had abandoned her. I chose to ignore her. After all, she was lonely and bitter and her lashing out was understandable—understandable, *not* acceptable.

A little while later Charlie arrived with lunch. I was glad because I was hungry and I knew Barbara Jean was. I was looking out the window when Charlie arrived. Much to my surprise my mother spoke to him first.

"Charlie, I sho' hope you got some good Mex'can food in dat bag."

"As a matter of fact, Ms. Jackson, I do."

"Don't call me that. I'm not old," she scolded him.

"Yes Ma' . . . I mean yes Barbara." He placed her food on her serving tray and placed it in front of her. He explained everything that he had purchased for her. He then handed me a carryout dish.

"And, a chimichanga smothered in hot green chili for the queen," he said to me. My mother coughed. Both of us ignored her. The chimichanga was delicious. That was another thing I missed about San Diego—good, authentic Mexican food. Often times, I would hire a group from a restaurant in Mexico to come across the border and grill carne asada on our patio. It seemed to help with morale in the office. The food was awesome.

After we ate, Charlie informed me that he had to meet Stuart at the Cherry Creek office for a meeting. He kissed me on the cheek and to my surprise, did the same to Barbara Jean.

After Charlie left the room, Barbara Jean looked at me with question in her eye.

"What?" I asked.

"Nothin'. Nothin' at all."

"Good," I said, not wanting to egg her on. I turned the television to her favorite soap opera in hopes to keep her busy. I could have gone into the office with Charlie and Stuart, but I couldn't concentrate on work and I wanted to make sure I was there when the doctor gave Barbara Jean's discharge instructions.

A few months earlier, Charlie had given me an iPod to listen to music while I was on the treadmill. Stuart and I had a stereo system in our workout room, but since I liked my music loud and with lots of bass, I didn't always use it. Stuart worked from home a lot and I didn't want to disturb or distract him. I had never seen anything like the neat little contraption before. It was half the size of a deck of cards and held hundreds of songs. It had earplugs so that I could listen to all the music my heart desired without disturbing anyone.

I placed the ear buds in my ear, and switched to one of my play lists. Joe's *I Wanna Know* was the first on my list. I reclined my chair, made sure Barbara Jean was okay and then I closed my eyes and lost myself in the music. After Joe came Yolanda Adam's *Open My Heart*.

I must have been sleep for a while because my current play list had reached song number fifty-two, which was Elton John's *Candle in the Wind*. It seemed as if Elton and someone else was calling my name until I realized my mother was calling me.

"Renee, wake up. Renee . . . Wake up. Renee!"

I finally realized that I wasn't dreaming and opened my eyes. Dr. Abrams was standing my mother's bed. I looked at my watch and realized it was after four o'clock.

"I didn't mean to sleep so long," I said.

"It's quite alright," Dr. Abrams said. "It can't be too comfortable sleeping in that chair. The good news is, I will have a nurse come in to check your mother's vitals and if her blood pressure is stabilized, she can go home shortly."

"How long is shortly," Barbara Jean asked.

"An hour tops," he responded.

"Thank God. No offense docta, but I can't wait to get outta hea' and I really don't care if I eva see you again."

"Tell me how you really feel," he chuckled. I shook the doctor's hand and thanked him for everything.

"She's going to need to come back three times a week for radiation. We're going to forgo the chemo. It's useless at this point. She will also need to attend physical therapy four times a week. I've compiled a list of home health care agencies that will accept her insurance so that she can have round the clock care." He turned to Barbara Jean, "Good luck little lady, and take care of yourself."

"You got any last minute advice docta?" she asked him.

"Yes. In fact I do. You may feel good, but your prognosis is the same. My advice is to party like its 1999 while you still have the chance."

As Dr. Abrams was leaving, a nurse came in to take my mother's vitals and draw more blood. Her blood pressure was still stable and she was given the okay to go home. I signed all the necessary paperwork, made necessary appointments and made sure all her things were packed and ready to go by the time Stuart came to pick us up.

I looked at Barbara Jean. She appeared to be back to her old self. She was going to be alright after all. She was healed and free to live her life like she had—or change it for the better. God had given her a second chance . . . healed her soul.

Chapter 13

I wanted to go to Barbara Jean's before she was released to clean her apartment and buy groceries for the fridge, but I obeyed Stuart who told me that he would help me once she was released. He said that I hadn't been taking care of the baby or myself since I'd been here and he would help me get things in order.

One of the nurses wheeled Barbara Jean down to our rental truck in a wheelchair and helped Stuart get her into the front seat. Stuart shut her door and we were off to Montbello to my mother's apartment.

"You know, if yall buy me a house, I would be a lil' mo' comfortable."

"I bet you would," I said. She never let up. For as long as I had been alive, Barbara Jean had been about money. One time I brought a boyfriend to meet her and she introduced herself as Barbara Jean Money and told him to never forget it. I chuckled at that thought.

"What's funny babe?" Stuart asked me looking through the rearview mirror.

"Just had a funny thought," I said. I could see him looking at me through the rearview mirror expecting an explanation. My eyes darted from the mirror to the back of my mother's head and back to the mirror. He understood.

When we arrived at my mother's apartment, I unlocked the door while Stuart helped her out of the car. When I opened the door, the stench hit my nose and nearly knocked me out the door. I knew I should have come before hand and cleaned. I opened all the windows and left the door open. I went back to her bedroom and was amazed at how dirty it was. I cleared a path from the doorway to her bed and managed to find sheets to change her bed with. The sheets still had the price tag on them. I shook my head.

When I walked back to the front of the house, Barbara Jean was sitting in one of her peach, winged back chairs and Stuart grabbed her a bottle of water. She looked at him when he handed it to her.

"What?" he asked.

"I suggest you drink that water out of the bottle. Had you kept the house clean, we'd be able to find a clean glass. So until I can wash the dishes, I suggest you drink the water or go thirsty," I told her.

Stuart looked at me in confusion. I explained to him that Barbara Jean did not like drinking out of bottles, she *had* to have a glass. He gave Barbara Jean a blank stare.

"Where my oxygen?" she asked.

"You don't need that oxygen. You need to lie down and get some rest."

"I been layin' down the last two monfs. I don't want ta lay down."

"Well I need you to go into your room and watch television so I can get this house cleaned up. I'm going to be using ammonia and bleach and I don't need you inhaling any of these fumes."

Stuart laughed at me. I assumed he had remembered the time I had mopped the bathroom floor with both bleach and ammonia. I turned my head for one moment and when I looked back into the bathroom, the room was full of smoke and the fire alarm had gone off.

"Don't you know you can blow us up with that concoction?" he asked before taking me out of the house. Hey, I figured it would get the floor "doubly" clean.

Stuart helped Barbara Jean back to her bedroom where the only television in the house resided. Since I had been born, Barbara Jean had never allowed a television in the living room and her children were never allowed there either.

Stuart left Barbara Jean in her room and came to help me clean the house.

"You know I'm not letting you use those chemicals around my baby right?" he said. I agreed and settled on Pine-Sol, even though I hated the smell.

I could hear Barbara Jean moving around. I was sure she was getting reacquainted with her things. Stuart and I dug in and began cleaning the mess before us.

I couldn't believe that my mother lived in such filth. Her expensive paintings and furniture were covered with dust and grease. There were burnt pots and pans sitting in the kitchen sink growing mold, and there were items in her fridge that should have been thrown out months ago.

Stuart and I started in the front room and worked our way to the back of her apartment. I dusted, polished, washed, degreased, and scrubbed, while Stuart vacuumed and mopped. I was startled when I opened her laundry pantry and clothes piled up to my chest fell out at me. It made no sense for one person to have this many clothes, and dirty to boot. The smell of mold attacked my nose as nausea took over. There were clothes that still had price tags on them. I had no idea what she planned on doing with this mess.

I began preparing clothes for Stuart and me to take to the laundromat. I would wash the clothes that I could manage to save and threw away those that I could not. There was no way my mother needed all these clothes so I began to prepare boxes for homeless shelters.

When I finally got to the bottom of the pile, I could see the source of the mildewed mess. The apartment manager later told me that Barbara Jean's laundry pantry was next to the boiler room that served all the units on that particular cluster. The pipes had burst and water had flooded into her apartment.

I made my way to the bathroom, which truthfully was worse than the molded closet. I shook my head at how Barbara Jean frivolously spent her money on unnecessary things. I mean, who needed four bottles of the same hairspray or three tubes of the same color lipstick amongst other things? I packed more boxes to give away. I poured bleach in the toilet, in the tub, in the sink and mopped the floor. I had never seen anything so filthy. Soon the fumes overcame me, so I shut the bathroom door and Barbara Jean's bedroom door and escaped outside for some fresh air.

Stuart ordered me to stay outside and he would finish cleaning as soon as the fumes cleared. As I cleared my lungs, I sat in Stuart's lap, in a chair next to Barbara Jean's bedroom window. I could hear her talking on the phone but didn't want to ease drop, so Stuart and I decided to go grab something to eat. There was no way I was cooking tonight.

† † †

A few days later, Stuart and I were sitting outside my mother's apartment working on reports on our laptop. That's when I overheard her conversation.

"I thank she want me dead. She ain't gave me my medicine and I ain't ate for a week," she said to the person she was talking to on the phone. I was sure she wasn't talking about me, because my mother had eaten more since she had arrived home from the hospital than the law would allow. I got as close as I could to the window as not to be detected and listened.

"I can't believe she brought that molesta' and that white boy to my house. She thank she all that, flossin' my ex and that peckerwood on her arm. She just don't know, even though she wit' him, I was wit him first. And to that white boy, she gone always be a nigga. She's lazy and nasty. She ain't took no bath or showa since she been hea."

I sat there with my mouth open. I had taken a shower every day since I had been in Denver; I just refused to take one in *her* house. And, after cleaning her house, I can't believe she was calling *me* lazy *or* nasty. Me?

My blood began to boil. Barbara Jean was jealous of my relationships with Stuart and Charlie. *Especially Stuart.* She was jealous that I had found something she had never seemed to find. She had been bitter and lonely most of her life and she tried to steal any joy that I had.

Here I was about to marry a man who loved and adored me, not to mention, my best friend Charlie by my side. It was eating her alive. And now, she was on the phone lying on me and degrading me to a family member, after all I had done, after all I had given up to take care of her. I continued to listen.

"I wish she would jes' leave. You know some of my thangs done came up missin' and I'm thankin' 'bout callin' tha police on her."

If she was trying to push me away, she was doing a good job because I wasn't going to stay much longer and put up with her crap. She had nine brothers and sisters, another child, her mother and other family members that all lived in the same city as she—yet none of them were anywhere to be found. Hell, I lived eighteen hundred miles away and I'd given up everything to be here for her. I knew she despised me but I came anyway, because I knew how the others would treat her. Yet, I was the one she treated like trash.

I listened for about another fifteen minutes as my mother trashed me from one end to the other. I walked upstairs to change a load of clothes in the washer with Stuart hot on my tail.

"I want to go home," I told him.

"Just say when and it is done," he said. We discussed the conversation we had just overheard and were sure that there probably had been more like them. Stuart was ready to wisp me away, but I convinced him to give me a little more time. Perhaps I would try harder. Perhaps that would make a difference.

I gave Stuart a list of items I needed for Barbara Jean's apartment and he headed off to King Soopers and K-Mart. I re-entered the apartment and knocked on her bedroom door.

"Mom, are you still on the phone?" I asked her peeking into her bedroom. She was lying on her bed facing the television, pretending to be asleep. I tapped her on the shoulder and asked her if she was hungry.

"What time is it?" she asked.

"It's eleven thirty," I told her.

"Why you let me sleep so late!" she yelled.

"What do you mean? You've been up since eight o'clock." Barbara Jean had done a complete Sybil on me and at that moment, I remembered that her doctor had told me that she would have spells where she didn't remember anything or would act like a totally different person. I chalked up her recent behavior as such.

I got her out of bed and prepared her for her shower. I had ordered a special chair for the tub so she could sit down and safely shower. When I sat her down, she complained that she couldn't wash herself, so I ended up having to do it for her.

For the next few weeks, Barbara Jean would become more and more helpless and I would endure more conversations as she degraded me to various people.

† † †

I got up early to make sure I was at Barbara Jean's house before she woke up. I left Stuart sleeping and wished he would take my suggestion and head back to San Diego. Although he wouldn't admit it, this whole Barbara Jean situation was taking a toll on our relationship. Even so, he and Charlie swore to be by my side until the end. Stuart did advise me that if Barbara Jean continued with her evil antics, he would *make* me leave.

I let myself into Barbara Jean's apartment and made sure it was clean. I prepared her things for her morning bath. I checked in on her and she was sound asleep. I went into the kitchen and started breakfast. I hadn't heard her walk up behind me, and was startled when I turned around.

"You ready to eat?" I asked her.

"Where yo' honkey friend at?"

"When you're done eating, I'll have your shower ready," I said ignoring her last little comment. But that wasn't enough for her.

"You know he only want you 'cause you's an easy lay for him." She was really pissing me off, and I wasn't going to take too much more of it, illness or not.

"Well, I guess the jokes on you, mother. Charlie and I are just good friends."

120

"Yea that's what'chu want me ta b'lieve. I thank you sleepin' wit bofe of 'em. You got to be openin' yo' legs for him, cause ain't no man like him gone stick 'round for no reason. You got ta be doin' somethin' for him."

"Yes I am. I'm his friend. And as usual, it kills you to see someone care for me without me having to give them absolutely anything but friendship and companionship."

"You seem to fa'get, I made you who you is, so I know you."

"Correction mother, you made me who I was. Now, I'm nothing like you. I will never be anything like you."

"Then why you here Renee? I'll tell you, 'cause you can't make it without me. That's why you here."

I looked at my pathetic mother and said, "Look around you mother. Who else is here for you? You have nine brothers and sisters who haven't been here once since you've been home. You have a son who hasn't even called to see if you were still alive, and a mother who could care less if you were okay or not. So you tell me who needs who right now!" I screamed.

My mother smirked. She succeeded in what she set out to do, and that was to get under my skin. I left her in the dining room to her breakfast as I folded the many loads of clothes that I had washed in the days previous.

† † †

Barbra Jean received her first visit three weeks after she had come home from the hospital. Her brother Jessie Lee Jr., who was nicknamed Junior, had a card and stuffed animal in tow.

"How you feeling Barbara? he asked her.

"Oh, I'm doin' a'ight," she answered. Junior sat in the chair opposite my mother and attempted to carry a conversation with her. He started to talk about his recent divorce *and* engagement.

"I didn't even know you two had divorced." I interrupted in shock.

"Yea, but that was over a year ago," he explained. So many things had changed since I had left Colorado. I was really out of the loop as to what was going on. My uncle and I continued the conversation as Barbara Jean sat in silence. She began holding the left side of her head, and squinting her eyes.

"What's wrong mother?" I asked.

"My brain hurt," she said. I immediately became irritated and snapped at her.

"Barbara Jean, you had surgery on the other side." She then shifted her hand to the right side of her head and repeated her act for attention. I ignored her and continued my conversation with my uncle. Barbara Jean decided that she wasn't getting the desired result from the last attention attempt and tried yet another time.

This time she turned to my uncle as if he was a stranger.

"I know who Lucy Hall is," she said looking into the distance as if she had seen a ghost or a spirit float by. My uncle looked at her then at me in confusion. I rolled my eyes at her and continued with our conversation as if she wasn't in the room. My uncle joined in after shaking his head.

Once again, Barbara Jean said, "I know who Lucy Hall is. She my sista-n-law," she added. Junior became discouraged and couldn't take it any longer. He was sure her actions were a result of the brain tumor. I, on the other hand, knew different.

Later, after Junior had left, I confronted Barbara Jean. "Mother why did you do that?" I asked.

"Do what?"

"Pretend like you done lost your mind," I said.

"How you know I was pretendin'?" she asked me.

"Because you've been doing it every since you've been home." I replied snidely.

"Well I was just tryna see if I could trick him out."

"One day you're going to cry wolf and no one is going to come to your aid." I told her, rolling my eyes again and walking out of the room.

Slowly but surely, people began to visit my mother. It was kind of a relief, and allowed me to spend less time away from my mother and more time with Stuart.

I had just laid down for a nap when my cell phone rang. It was my mother's pastor. Reverend Burns said he had found a fill-in for Wednesday's bible study and he would give an hour of his time every Wednesday to have bible study at my mother's apartment. I raced to Barbara Jean's to make sure she was presentable.

When I opened the door, I could hear her talking to someone. I stood by her bedroom door and listened. She was having another degrading session and I was her main subject. I convinced myself that I wasn't going to let her bother me. Before I could warn her that Reverend Burns was on his way, the doorbell rang. It was Reverend Burns and his wife and a few other church members.

"It's Reverend Burns," I told her. Barbara Jean jumped up out of bed and ran to the bathroom.

This certainly could not be the helpless woman that could barely walk or speak I thought to myself.

I followed her to the bathroom and watched her as she put on her wig. The radiation and chemotherapy had taken most of her hair. She followed up with red lipstick and blush, made sure she had just enough cleavage showing and ran halfway down the hall to her walker. I shook my head as I watch my mother pretend to be frail and weak as she used her walker to assist her into the living room where her guests awaited her. I couldn't believe it. I left her alone with her guests, called Stuart from the spare room, and told him what I had just witnessed.

† † †

I finally got my mother to get out of the house and to church. All she could think about was what she was going to wear. She leaned on a walker she did not need and attempted to squeeze her overly swollen foot into a clear three-inch pump.

"You know you can't fit those, "I told her.

"But they match my blue outfit. This tough girl. This here is Donna Karin," she bragged in her sometimey *proper* voice.

"I don't care if it's Denzel Washington, it doesn't make any sense to me," I said pursing my lips. My mother always annoyed me with her designer *this* and designer *that* and would curse you to hell if you mentioned Wal-Mart.

I made sure she was dressed to the 'T', even with the low-heeled shoes I had substituted for the pumps she had previously chosen. I had gone the day before and fitted her for a nice fashionable wig. I did her hair and makeup, and before we knew it, we were on way down Interstate 70 en route to her church. I had purposely kept her walker in the trunk and out of sight. Her physical therapist had told her he didn't want her using it and only wanted her to get minimal use of her cane. However, Barbara Jean was insistent on using the walker. She said she was afraid of falling, and although that

124

may have been partially true, I knew the main reason my mother used that walker was to get attention.

My instinct proved true when we pulled into the parking lot of her church and she helped herself out of the car and around to the trunk better than I ever could have. I took her walker from the trunk and unfolded it. She carried it from the car to the entrance of the church, but as soon as she got to the entrance of the church, she rendered herself helpless once more, or as a friend of mine would say *"one moe again."*

The choir was singing when we got inside and once they saw Barbara Jean, they shouted *amens, hallelujas* and *thank you Jesus'*. Everyone rushed to her side. The scene nearly made me sick.

I made sure she was seated in the front row and I took residence in the row behind her. I noticed, as I sat down, that my mother's aunt was also seated on the front row. She didn't speak to me and I didn't speak to her. It was no secret that we did not like each other. Why she didn't particularly care for me, I didn't know and didn't care, but I gathered it was mostly because of erroneous information that she had gotten from my mother.

The church service moved smoothly with frequent notions on how good the Lord was by showing His awesome and wondrous abilities with blessings in the form of my mother.

After the service ended, we received a couple of dinner invitations from members of the congregation. Barbara Jean finally settled on the invitation to have dinner at her aunt's house. She knew that I would not go, but made a public plea for me to join her. I publicly declined. I told her to enjoy herself and to call me on my cell when she was ready to come home. I went back to the hotel and Stuart and I went out for dinner.

Later, Barbara Jean called to inform me that her aunt would be taking her home. I gave her a good head start before I headed towards her apartment. What happened when I got to her place sealed my decision to head back to San Diego. I was hoping that my great aunt had left, but to my disappointment, her car was in the parking lot when Stuart and I pulled up.

"I brought yo' mama home, since you found somethin' else betta to do," my great aunt said.

"What are you talking about? I told her to call me when she was ready to come home," I defended myself.

"I see ya mama was right about you bein' fat *and* a big liar," she attacked me. I looked at my mother as she pretended to be out of it. There was no way I was going to stand here and let this woman treat me this way and I was not going to let my mother get away with what she had started. What happens when you back a dog into a corner? He comes out fighting.

"Look here you old unattractive, country bitch. I don't know *who* you think you are, but I am not the one to be fucking with right now. Now I don't know what my mother told you, and I don't really care, but I suggest you check yourself before I put my foot in your ass." The more I talked the angrier I became. "And for the record, I happen to be pregnant. What's *your* excuse?" I reached back and tried to muster as much strength as I could to knock her ass out, but Stuart grabbed my arm.

"She's not worth it babe. None of this is." He looked to Barbara Jean and said, "Barbara Jean, you are going to have to find someone else to care for you. I'm taking my fiancé home. She deserves much better than this. I'm sorry for your situation, but I will no longer stand by and watch you try to destroy her." Stuart grabbed me by the waist and basically carried me out to the car. I was so ready to say goodbye to this God forsaken state and a family that I wanted no part of.

Chapter 14

Stuart and I drove back to the hotel in silence. He held my hand but kept his eyes on the road. We would get a good night's sleep and then head back to San Diego in the morning.

Part of me felt guilty leaving Barbara Jean behind, even with the way she had treated me. I knew no one was going to take better care of her. I knew everyone else, except for Eddie had an ulterior motive. But the fact still remained that I had to worry about my unborn baby. I would need to get to my doctor as soon as I got back for a checkup. I hadn't been eating right and I was under lots of stress. Stuart chimed in on my thoughts.

"It was just that, I couldn't stand the way she treated you. I mean, no one else stepped in to help, and here you were willing to give up your life and jeopardize the baby's health just to try to save hers and you got nothing in return. I can't allow that. Not on my watch."

I knew Stuart meant well, and he was right. But there was something in me that kept telling me that I should have stayed in spite of. A trip back down memory lane sucked me in.

Drifting . . .

Drifting . . .

Drifting . . .

My brother and I knew it was *that* time of the month. *That* time happened twice a month. That time when Barbara Jean's boyfriend, Hal, got paid. It was beyond me why he continued to carry on with this nonsense. For years, it had happened, just like a broken record, over and over again.

It was Hal's payday. Eddie and I knew the routine. Hal would get paid every other Friday, come home late that night, after doing God knows what with God knows who, and give Barbara Jean half his paycheck. It seemed to me that most women would die to get half of their man's paycheck on a regular basis—*not* Barbara Jean, she wanted it all. Hal knew this, but just like tax time was a definite each year, Hal was only going to give her half of his paycheck and he knew the consequences that came with *that* half.

He would come home reeking of alcohol, she would yell, fuss and fight and Eddie, and I would be summoned from our beds, from our sleep, to move Hal's belongings from the house and kindly place them in the middle of the street in front our house. Once the move had been performed, more yelling, cursing and screaming would take place, followed by Barbara Jean puncturing some part of Hal's body with a butcher knife.

This night was different—different because I was tired, not physically but mentally. I couldn't take it anymore. On this night, I would not comply with Barbara Jean's wishes, a deed that held a steep price for me.

After not achieving adequate satisfaction from stabbing Hal, *at least three times,* she summoned for our neighbors, three men, who had just moved in across the street, to come over and "handle" him. I gathered Barbara Jean's guess was a bit accurate, because I also doubted that Hal even felt the pain of the piercing blade any longer, but he sure wasn't going to stick around and be attacked by three grown men. His getaway was given to him by the unlocked back door, which he fled through and jumped over the back fence and into the night.

I stood in the doorway of my room as Eddie sat in his bed crying, with the covers over his head. What I heard next sickened me.

"I need help! My boyfriend attack me. I thank I been stabbed."

Silence.

"I don't know, he smell like he was drankin'."

Silence.

She had to stop, pant, and then slow down her speech to make it more believable.

"Please herry up, I'm disable and I'm bleedin' real bad." She placed the phone on its cradle and laid on the floor close to the cracked front door.

Within minutes, police sirens could be heard as they turned onto our street and pulled in front of our house. A group of firemen and two police officers arrived at the same time.

"Is everyone alright in here?" the officer asked, as he held his gun with one hand and carefully pushed the front door open softly, as not to injure Barbara Jean who lay sprawled on the floor.

"I don't know, I thank I done been stabbed. He tried ta' kill me." She put on the theatrics thick, as only she knew how. They came with great sound effects—moaning, panic attacks and screaming.

"I'm bleedin'! I'm bleedin'! Oh, help me oh Lord. Don't let me die!"

"Ma'am, what happened?" the officer asked her.

"He was drunk. And he came home and started beatin' on me. My kids saw the whole thang."

The officer looked up and noticed Eddie and me standing in the doorway of our bedroom. He walked toward us.

"Are you both alright?" he asked, speaking to whichever one of us that would answer. Eddie stepped back into the dark bedroom in silence. The look on Barbara Jean's face behind the officer told him that he had better go along with the plan. She shot me the same look. I didn't move.

"I need to know what happened here," the officer attempted once more.

"I'll tell you what happened." I finally spoke. "Every pay day, we go through the same thing. We've gone through it for years. If you don't believe me, check your police records. They will tell you how many times you've actually been here." I told the officer of times past and gave him the details of what happened that night.

"And after he left, she called you guys, and then she laid down on the floor and pretended like she was hurt." The officer looked from me, to Eddie and then to my mother's oxygen tank that sat nearby.

"Oh don't be fooled by that either. She put it on right before you got here. She doesn't really need it and only uses it so she can continue to get her social security and disability check." If my mother had a gun, she would have shot me right then and there, but unfortunately, for me, her look sufficed.

"I'm so sick and tired of going through this. And then, I don't understand him. He's the stupid one. You'd think that he'd either just give her the entire check or just never come back. Each time, we have to put his clothes out in the street only to have to go back out and get what's left the next morning and bring it back into the house."

I knew that if this police officer did not take me with him, when he left our house that night, Barbara Jean would make me pay dearly . . . but I was on a roll.

"And that's not even her blood. Check her out. She wasn't stabbed. *She* stabbed *him*. It's *his* blood." By this time, Eddie was back in his bed crying loudly. He knew that as soon as the police left, I would surely meet my demise. Much to my surprise, when the officers, the firemen and the paramedics left, Barbara Jean didn't come after me . . . physically.

"You ungrateful lil' bitch," she said as she stood in front of me. "Get'cho ass out my house right now! After all I done did for yo' ass. You get the hell out now!" I went to retrieve my shoes from my closet but she stopped me.

"You ain't buy shit in hea' and you ain't gone take nothin' wit' you. You get out and get out now, before I kill you!"

Barefoot and clothed in my pajamas, I walked out of my mother's house and into the cold night, with nowhere to go. I decided I would walk to my best friend's house.

When I knocked on the door my best friend's stepfather let me in.

"Girl where are your shoes?" he asked.

"She did it again dad." I told him. He was "dad" to all the children in the neighborhood who didn't have one.

"I'm so sick of this," he said as he disappeared into a bedroom and reappeared with a pair of shoes and a coat for me. "Let's go. We're going to straighten this out." I didn't want to go back there. I knew there was no working anything out and the end result would warrant yet another beating.

We drove back to Barbara Jean's house. I stayed in the car while my play dad knocked on our front door.

"Barbara Jean, what is going on? And why is this child out here in the middle of the night with no coat or shoes on?"

"I put her out," Barbara Jean said with boldness.

"Does that make any sense?" he asked her.

"Go back home to yo' wife and stay out my business," she told him.

"This *is* my business, when this baby shows up at my door after midnight, with no shoes or coat on. It's damn near forty-five degrees outside."

"Where is she?" I heard Barbara Jean inquire.

"In the car," he responded. I saw her look towards the car. I rolled up the window as fast as I could. Barbara Jean ran towards the car.

"Get yo' ass out tha' car!" she yelled.

"I know you don't expect her to get out while you're yelling at her," my play dad told her.

"I only wanna talk to huh," Barbara Jean said. I sat there frozen thinking to myself that it was a trap, praying he didn't open the car door. After Barbara Jean calmed down and convinced my play dad she only wanted to talk, he summoned me to get out of the car.

"But she is going to whip me," I protested.

"No I ain't," she said.

"Do you promise?" I asked for reassurance. I knew I was pushing it, but I felt like I had half a chance with "dad" there.

"I promise I ain't gone whip you." I reluctantly got out of the car. Barbara Jean and my play dad did most of the talking and I did most of the listening. Somehow, my play dad, believed most of what my mother was saying. Once he was convinced, he kissed me on the cheek, watched me go into the house and drove away.

When I went into my room, I was startled by a painful sting on my neck and my back.

"You promised you wouldn't whip me!" I cried.

"I'm not gone to whip you, I'm gone beat tha hell outta yo' black ass!" she said in a range that startled me. She struck me for what seemed like a hundred more times with an extension cord.

"If you eva . . . pull . . . some . . . shit . . . . like . . . that . . . Imma . . . kill . . . you," she said pausing and taking a deep breath in between each blow. Luckily, for me, she finally became exhausted.

I lay on the floor where she left me, sobbing and trying to stop the blood flow of a few open welts on my body. What hurt more than my aching, burning and bruised body was Eddie's silence through the entire ordeal.

"Babe. Babe!" I finally heard Stuart say. "Are you alright?"

"Just a bit lost in thought. Did you call Charlie to let him know we're headed back to California?"

"Yes. He's catching the red eye and said he'd see us once we returned. I've already got us booked for a flight at 7:47 in the morning. Is that okay?"

"Yes, that's fine. The sooner I can leave this god awful place, the better."

He pulled me close to him and I nestled my face in the nape of his neck. He always smelled so good. I let out a loud sigh. He rubbed my belly.

"When was the last time you fed my baby?" he asked.

"When we went out to lunch," I was ashamed to say. Stuart made sure that I kept fruit and a few fresh vegetables in the fridge at the hotel and in Barbara Jean's fridge. I was so stressed out that I completely forgot.

"That's okay. When we get back, I'm going to take care of that. You're going to work from home."

I looked at him like he had lost his mind. Before I could interject, he interrupted me.

"Look. Put Denver behind you. You have two people to think about now. We don't need any problems with the baby.

If it makes you feel better, you can go into the office once a week."

He had spoken. I wouldn't give him a hard time about it. Besides, I was tired, both physically and mentally. Once I got back home, I would sleep for at least a week.

The next morning we showered and headed to the airport. We dropped off our rental car and headed to the gate. Before we boarded the plane, I looked back and gave Denver one last look. I had no intentions of ever returning. Of course, I thought the same when I left Denver the first time. I knew a few people in Southern California who had left their embarrassment of a home life, moved to California and changed everything from their appearances to their names. I had given it a bit of thought, but came to the conclusion that although I would always strive to be a better person, I would not change my name.

At times, I was embarrassed of my past, but realized that is was my past that had made me the strong independent woman I was today.

Although Barbara Jean wasn't my favorite person, one day I'd thank her for how she treated me. If it had not been for how she had raised me, I wouldn't be who I was today. And I was pretty happy with the person I had become. Not only was I financially stable, I had friendship and love all around me. And to top it off, God had brought me the man of my dreams. I had to admit that I was pretty blessed and I actually felt content.

I had to wonder about Barbara Jean. Part of me felt so sorry for her. I cried when I thought about how she raised me. I cried even harder trying to imagine Barbara Jean enduring the abuse of her father, my grandfather. Not be able to go to school and learn, to have to help with the other children in the family, while being a child herself. My anger suddenly focused on Memah. The thought of my grandmother standing idly by while her husband mentally and physically violated her daughter. How can a mother do that and live with herself?

I rubbed my stomach. I would be different. I've heard many psychologists on talk shows and other venues say that a child grows up to be a prototype of their parents. I disagreed. I loved Stuart, but I'd kill him dead if he even *thought* about touching my daughter in a harmful way. I would show my children every day how much I loved them and I would tell them.

No, I wasn't a product of my environment, I was better than my past. Yes, it helped mold me, but I would not carry on the generational curse that black families tend to carry from generation to generation.

Neither me, nor Barbara jean were the *only* instances of our family secrets.

All throughout my childhood, I was told that we don't air our dirty laundry, nor do we tell on family. Humph. I had to chuckle a bit because ten years after my uncle had raped me, Barbara Jean had the nerve to tell me that *she* was ready to deal with it and she wanted to take it to Oprah. She wasn't about to profit from *my* misfortune.

I remembered another instance where my cousin Shayla was raped by the very same uncle that had raped me. This time, he had caught my cousin off guard outside the bank she had worked at and violated her at gunpoint.

When I got word, I wanted to be there for her, but her mother refused to allow me to talk to her. Shayla was so distraught that she never trusted men again and began looking to women for love.

My aunt Susan had called me a couple of years ago and told me that the family was being disgraced again because

Shayla revealed that she was a lesbian. The sad thing about it was, no one faulted our uncle for what he had done, and to this day, he walks freely, mingling with the family as if nothing ever happened.

No, I wanted no part of that type of family. I didn't need it, and I didn't need them. I would make a name for myself as Stuart's wife, the mother of his children, and one of the best stockbrokers the west had ever seen.

Chapter 15

I was so happy to be back in San Diego, I never wanted to leave again. A car picked us up from the airport and drove us home. When Stuart opened the front door, a stench attacked our noses. I immediately knew its source. I had forgotten to dispose of certain dairy products in the fridge. I hadn't expected to be gone as long as we were.

Immediately a wave of nausea came over me as I headed to my office and shut the door. Stuart opened a few windows and the patio door to the eat-in section of the kitchen. He cleaned the fridge and soon the sour smell began to dissipate.

I wanted to check my messages, but decided against it. The answering machine's LED indicator read *22 new messages*. I knew if it said I had twenty-two messages, my tape was full and several other messages did not make it on the tape. I booted my computer, but before the *Windows 2000* welcome screen could disappear on my screen, Stuart was standing in the doorway.

"Babe, you really need to get some rest. That can wait until tomorrow." He was right. I knew once I became enthralled in my work, I'd be sitting there for hours working until I fell asleep at my desk.

I decided that I would call my obstetrician and make an appointment for a checkup. I was already scheduled for a couple of appointments but missed them while in Denver. I had meant to find a doctor in Colorado to visit, but dealing with Barbara Jean caused me to forget about everything, including the health of my baby.

I contacted my doctor and was able to get an appointment the next day. I was relieved. I rubbed my belly and asked my unborn child for forgiveness.

"I'm wondering if these stairs are going to be a problem," Stuart said as he helped me up them and to the bedroom. Charlie had picked the house out so I really had no say so in it. I fell in love with it the first time I saw it—and stairs and *babies* were the *last* things on my mind.

The air was much better once we reached the master bedroom. Stuart opened the windows anyway to let the wonderful breeze that was flowing from the ocean come through the window. I undressed and put on a set of silk pajamas. I had no intentions of leaving the house for the rest of the day.

Stuart disappeared, only to reappear moments later with a small plate of fruit and orange juice.

"I know it's not much, but you need to feed the baby. I didn't want to give you anything too heavy for fear you'd become nauseous again."

"Thank you. You're so thoughtful." I was back in my element and happy as a Bessie bug.

After I ate most of the fruit and drank most of the juice, I laid across the bed and covered myself with a throw. Before I knew it, I was out like a light.

† † †

I was awakened by the sound of the telephone ringing. After the third ring, Stuart appeared in the doorway.

"It's Charlie, do you feel like talking?"

"Sure," I responded. Stuart handed me the cordless phone.

"Hi Charlie. How are you doing?"

"Doing great Luv. How are you doing?"

"Exhausted."

"I can imagine. You've been through a lot the last few weeks and you haven't been taking care of yourself."

"I know, but I'm home now. You have no idea how happy I am."

"Ah, I think I have an idea. Please . . . rest and I'll check on you later."

"Thanks Charlie."

"You're welcome Luv. Can you put Stu on the line?" I did as I was told and called out to Stuart to pick up the phone. Once he did, I clicked off the cordless receiver. I went to the cove in our master bedroom to get a bottle of water from the mini-fridge.

As I bent down to open the door, I felt a sharp pain shoot through my abdomen—right before I fell to the floor. Something didn't feel right. At first, I thought it was a bad case of gas . . . until I felt my clothes get wet. I wanted to get to the bathroom but couldn't move. I positioned myself into a fetal position and that's when I saw the blood. I hollered out for Stuart. The pain got worse.

"Oh God, please no," I said out loud. I couldn't be losing my baby. I called to Stuart again, but this time, my cry was barely audible. The Lord heard my cry and intervened because Stuart came running into the bedroom like a bat out of hell.

"Baby? What's wrong?" he asked.

"The . . . baby," I said in short deep breaths. Stuart immediately dialed 911, while trying to calm me down. The 911 operator on the other end tried to calm Stuart, down but she was unsuccessful. Luckily for me, I could hear sirens in the distance and getting closer. I managed to convince Stuart to go downstairs to let in the paramedics. In just few short minutes later, two paramedics were at my side and lifting me onto a stretcher.

"Be careful with her and my baby," Stuart warned them

"Is she pregnant sir?" they asked him.

"Yes, about six months or so," he responded.

The male paramedic spoke into his walkie-talkie. "Possible miscarriage."

"No!" I shrieked. Stuart held my hand telling me to calm down as he tried to assure me that everything was going to be okay. How could he think I was okay? I was bleeding and the pain hadn't subsided. All of a sudden, I got dizzy and then . . . everything went . . . black.

I opened my eyes and was startled by bright lights. I looked around and realized I was in a hospital. I looked to my left and saw Stuart sitting in a chair. He was sound asleep. I knew he was tired and had gotten very little sleep the last few weeks. I didn't dare wake him.

"There she is," Dr. Chow sang as he pulled back the curtain. That woke Stuart. He was up and instantly at my side. He held my hand and kissed it as we listened to Dr. Chow's diagnosis.

"I'm not a very happy doctor at this moment Renee," he said. "You were given special instructions to take it easy and stay away from stressful situations."

"In my defense doctor, my mother has cancer. And she's a handful."

"Oh, I'm sorry to hear that. Still, you have another person to think of besides yourself. The baby looks fine but I'm afraid that another visit to the ER could cause you to lose the baby."

"Don't worry Doctor," Stuart said, not taking his eyes off me. "I can guarantee you, this will *not* happen again." I was defeated. Who was I to interject?

Dr. Chow explained that he wanted to keep me in the hospital overnight for observation and I should be able to go home the next day. I convinced Stuart to leave my side and find something to eat.

When I was alone, I thanked God for taking care of me and saving my baby. I couldn't help think about Barbara Jean. If what her doctor said was true, I would have to visit Denver at least one more time. I didn't know how to break that Stuart. I decided not to bring it up until I received that call . . .*if* I received that call. I genuinely wondered how Barbara Jean was holding up.

I disliked hospitals with a passion and I couldn't wait for Dr. Chow to come in to discharge me. I was hungry and it was apparent that the baby was hungry as well. I pulled my hospital gown to the side to show Stuart. My stomach looked as if it was possessed as the baby moved around.

"He can't wait to get out of there can he?"

"Or *she*," I said.

"He *or* she. Does that hurt when the baby moves around like that?"

"Not at all. It just feels strange."

"God is an awesome God isn't He?"

"Yes he is. To think how a baby is created is miraculous. And the growing process of a baby, to a child, to a grown up. Whew! That is so awesome. Umph, umph, umph." I shook my head. I was in disbelief every time I stopped to look at one of God's creations . . . so surreal.

A duty nurse came in to get my vital signs and give me discharge instructions. She instructed me that Dr. Chow would be in shortly. I was relieved, because at that moment, I wanted to be at home in my nice comfortable bed.

"Do you want me to set up one of the rooms downstairs so you don't have to climb the stairs?" Stuart asked me. Just then, Dr. Chow walked into the room.

"I think that would be a great idea, Mr. Humphries. Even though Renee only has a few more weeks until delivery, she can still have complications if she doesn't take it easy."

"You don't have to worry about that doctor, I'll make sure she's a good girl."

With that, Dr. Chow discharged me and Stuart and I headed home.

† † †

I relaxed in the oversized chair in the great room while Stuart prepared one of guest rooms. I went through the large pile of mail that was delivered while we were gone.

The doorbell rang once and then I heard keys in the lock. It had to be Charlie. I felt a little uneasy because I had expressed to Charlie that he could no longer just walk into the house now that Stuart and I were together.

"Hello," I heard him say from the great room.

"She's in the den," I heard Stuart call out.

Charlie entered the great room with a dozen roses and a teddy bear. He kissed me on the forehead.

"How's the patient doing?"

"I'm good," I answered and looked behind him. He knew what I was thinking.

"I called Stu before I came and he told me it was okay to come in. Is that okay with *you*?"

I was a little relieved. "Of course. So, how is my best friend doing?"

"I don't think you should say that out loud. Stuart might not like you calling me that."

"You two are funny," Stuart said, joining us. He and Charlie exchanged pleasantries and hugs.

Chapter 16

I looked over at the caller ID when the phone rang. It was Susan. I could feel my muscle tense up.

"Hello?" I answered.

"Renee?"

"What's wrong? I asked her. I could tell by her voice that all was not well with Barbara Jean.

"You need to get your mother out of here as soon as you can."

"Why?"

"Lester is trying to put her in a nursing home," she said. Everyone knew that if Barbara Jean were taken out of her element, she would go down fast. She was very materialistic and her apartment showed it. If she were taken from that element, both her mental *and* physical health would suffer.

"You know if they put her in a nursing home, she's not coming out," I told Susan.

"I know, that's why *you* have to do something."

"What is everyone else doing? I can't do much from here. I'm on bed rest. Besides, I have been trying to call her and every time I do, Lester answers the phone and hangs up."

"Hold on, I'm going to do a three way," she said. She switched over, dialed my mother's number then clicked back over to my line.

"Who this?" Lester answered.

"Susan," my aunt said. "How's Barbara Jean?"

"She doin' a'right. You wanna talk to her?"

"Yes. When are you taking her to the nursing home," she asked.

"It's a hospice," he corrected her. I wanted to curse him every which way but loose, but I knew if he knew I was on the line, he'd hang up.

"Hello?"

"Barbara Jean, it's Susan."

"Hey Susan. How you?"

"I have Renee on the other end of the phone, but you can't let Lester know," she warned her.

"Hello mother," I said.

"Hey. What you doin'?" she asked me.

"Trying to get you down here," I told her.

"Barbara Jean, we need to get you down to San Diego with Renee, because tomorrow Lester is going to put you in a nursing home," Susan told her.

"I gotta talk to my docta first," she responded.

I jumped in. "I've already talked to your doctor. He has already cleared you and thinks you would have a better chance at survival if you move from the smog and come here."

"Well Lester done said I can't come stay wit' you, 'cause you was gone leave me dead on tha beach." That was all that had to be said. Lester got on the phone and started cursing.

"You bastard, you know if you put her in a nursing home, she is going to die," I yelled at him.

"I don't see you here," he retorted.

"I *was* there and you all couldn't seem to mind your own damn business. You wanted to be the one to run things. But it back fired. You thought if you forced Barbara Jean on your wife, she would be so busy taking care of Mom that she wouldn't have time to worry about you doing your dirt."

I was heated at this point. He brought the ugly out in me and I wasn't going to let him off the hook that easily.

"You've already convinced her to turn her money over to you, just like you did the first time. You don't care about her, you just want her money. I will be there to get my mother and I hope you are there when I get there." I ended the call.

Part of me wanted to call Eddie and have him put a hit out on Lester, but I decided against it. I knew had I done so, Eddie would have followed through.

Lucky for me Stuart was at the office. I wasn't positive, but I could literally feel my blood pressure rise. My face began to burn and I was becoming angrier by the moment. The baby started kicking and moving—a reminder that I needed to bring it down a notch.

I took a deep breath and decided to get out of my office and to sit out on the back patio with a cup of tea. I took in the atmosphere. The back patio was covered and to my right was a water feature with beautiful landscaping.

Straight ahead, a path gave way to one of the most beautiful ocean scenes I had ever witnessed. Charlie came to mind. He knew me better than anyone else . . . including Stuart. Even though he picked this house for me, he made sure every little detail had me in mind.

The air was a bit cool and the breeze that grazed the water sent dew into my face. It felt so wonderful. I took in the moment of peace and closed my eyes. I tried to take my mind off Barbara Jean for a moment and tried to focus on the things I had to do to prepare for the baby's arrival. I was relieved that Charlie had suggested that Sonja come down to help me out.

Sonja was a Godsend. She had turned one of the bedrooms upstairs into a nursery. She painted the walls a universal green.

We didn't know the sex of the baby, so we wanted to make sure whatever color we chose, it would fit a boy or a girl.

Sonja had ordered a dark cherry ensemble, along with all the bells and whistles. She chose a Care Bear theme and hung a Care Bear mobile above the bed. The room was complete with a crib, moveable basinet, changing table and plenty of storage space. Sonja went a bit overboard with baby toys. Much of what she had purchased, the baby would not be able to utilize for a while.

"Señora Renee, this is your first child. We are going to spoil this bambino." I could have sworn that she was just as excited as I was. I appreciated her help and her friendship.

I heard the security alarm chime from the inside of the house. I looked at my watch. It was three o'clock. I hadn't expected Stuart until six. Luckily, Sonja had fixed dinner.

Stuart joined me on the patio. "Hey babe," he said, kissing me on the lips.

"Hey babe. How was your day?"

"Pretty good. Everyone said to tell you hello and they can't wait until you have the baby, so they can spoil it."

I smiled. As quiet as it was kept, I missed being in the office and in the midst of the chaos of Wall Street. I missed my co-workers and the human interaction.

Stuart looked at me for a minute, then asked, "You sure you're okay?"

I raised my eyebrow. "Yes, why do you ask?"

"I got a call from Susan."

I rolled my eyes and took a deep breath. How dare she call my fiancé. Suddenly the anger I felt earlier had returned.

"You're not worrying yourself with this are you? Because I know Barbara Jean is your mother, but what's important to me is *you* and our baby. And I hate to say this, but, if saving

Barbara Jean means sacrificing my family's health, then Barbara Jean is on her own. I'm sorry, but that's how I feel and I'm standing by my feelings."

He didn't need to apologize. I knew exactly how he felt. I just didn't want to have to answer to God if I hadn't lifted a hand to help her. But, then again, I had. I was only human and could only do so much.

"I offered to let her live with us, but Lester is not going to let that happen. He's afraid that if she comes here, he won't get the money she left him in her will."

"When did *we* decide that it was okay for Barbara Jean to stay with us?" he asked. I didn't respond. I stared off into the beauty of the ocean. I still hadn't gotten used to the fact that I needed to clear things with the man I would soon call my husband. I knew I was wrong. Stuart rubbed me on my shoulder and disappeared into the house. I knew I had overstepped my bounds and felt bad.

I knew how he felt about Barbara Jean and the entire situation, but at the same time, I wish he would understand that she was still my mother and guilt wouldn't let it go. However, the bottom line was, if Stuart said she couldn't stay, she couldn't stay.

I stayed outside for a bit longer. I needed peace. I didn't want to see disappointment in Stuart's eyes. I didn't want to deal with other people's financial situations. I didn't want to deal with plans for the baby and I didn't want to deal with Barbara Jean right now. I wrapped a throw around my torso, snuggled into the seat, and closed my eyes.

I began talking to God seeking answers. We talked for what seemed like hours before I finally dozed off.

† † †

149

The chill in the air woke me. It was now dark as I looked at my watch. It was nine o'clock in the evening. It was evident by the extra blanket on me that Stuart had been out to check on me. I sat there for a moment looking into the darkness. I felt somewhat refreshed. Now, I had to go back in and face my fiancé.

When I went inside, I didn't see Stuart *or* Sonja. I went into the kitchen and turned on the microwave. Sonja had saved my dinner there. When the microwave beeped, Sonja came into the kitchen.

"Señora, when you are finished eating, I would like to show you something." I decided to wait on dinner and followed Sonja to the baby's nursery.

I stopped in the doorway, and looked up at the ceiling. Sonja had taken a portrait that Stuart and I had recently taken that exposed my baby bump and painted it on the ceiling. I hadn't realized that Sonja was so talented.

"So when the bambino looks up, he *or* she can see the mobile *and* mommy and daddy. What do you think?"

"I think its beautiful Sonja. Why am I just now finding out about your talent?"

"I cannot say Señora. You know the portrait of the flowers in Señor Charlie's dining room?" I nodded. "I painted that."

"Wow." I was amazed. I had complimented Charlie several times on his taste in choosing the painting and never once did he mention that it was Sonja's handy work.

"Why aren't you doing this for a living?" I asked her.

"I do private pieces for special customers. Señor Charlie has tried to talk me into opening a gallery, but I don't know if I want that responsibility."

"I think you would do *so* well. You are a true talent. And I don't say that to just anybody." She smiled at me.

"What's all the commotion?" Stuart asked when he joined us in the nursery.

"Look at what Sonja has done," I said pointing to the ceiling.

"Wow." Stuart was just as impressed as I was. "And what exactly is the reason you choose to be a housekeeper and assistant?"

"Family. Señor Charlie, you and Señora Renee are family to me. I wouldn't trade that for anything."

I hugged Sonja. She was right, she *was* family to us.

I headed back to the kitchen to eat the delicious dinner that Sonja had prepared. I took a bite of the smothered burritos and rolled my eyes into the back of my head. It was delicious. That woman could cook her butt off.

Stuart joined me in the kitchen. "I'm sorry for earlier. If you want Barbara Jean to come stay, she can stay with us. I want you to know, I *do* understand. "

"No, *I'm* sorry. I still have to get used to this *us* thing and realize it is no longer just about me. I should have talked to you first. You are going to be my husband and if you don't want her here, I will respect that. My first priority is to you and our baby." We embraced for a quick moment.

"Since I'm the man of the house, I need you to stop eating that spicy food until after the baby is born," he smirked. I looked at him and then down at my belly. Just then, the baby started kicking. I gathered the plate in my hand and turned my back towards Stuart. I devoured every morsel on my plate before he decided to confiscate my meal. I could hear him laugh behind me.

"Sonja!" he called out.

"Si Señor?" she answered.

"No more spicy food for the lady of the house until after the baby, ¿Comprende?"

"Comprendo señor."

"¡Conspiración!" We all let a bout of laughter.

Chapter 17

I sat in my home office observing my ticker monitors. The markets were still reacting to the September 11th attacks. Analysts were calling it a corrective bear market.

I had my office line forwarded to my home office and my phone was ringing off the hook. I spent a while trying to convince my clients not to panic. I instructed them on what investments to liquidate and which ones not to.

The Federal Reserve Chairman, Alan Greenspan was on television now. I was trying to listen to him and to one of my clients at the same time. She wanted to sell her entire portfolio. I advised that it would be the biggest financial mistake that she'd make. After the call was done, I was able to stop her from selling those securities that I was sure would get her through her retirement years.

Things began to calm down after Greenspan, whom we'd affectionately nicknamed E.F. Hutton, finished his press conference. However, there were still many worrywarts out there making the biggest mistakes of their lives.

The Eastern Standard Time clock struck four o'clock and the closing bell rang. I was so glad because I didn't want to take another phone call. That didn't mean my phone stopped ringing. I pressed the voice mail button, routing all incoming calls to voice mail, with the option to press zero for a menu of other options.

I sat back in my chair and felt something wet on my pants leg. I looked down and found that my pants were soaked and they were getting wetter by the minute. Had I just sat her and urinated on myself? Then in an instant, I panicked.

"Sonja!" I yelled. Within seconds, Sonja was in my office.

"Si Señora. What is the matter?"

"I think my water just broke!"

"Calm down Señora. We do just as we practiced okay?" Sonja was calm and it irritated me, but I let her take control. She called 9-1-1, Stuart, and then Charlie. She told them to meet us at the hospital and within minutes, I was being transported by ambulance to the hospital.

Here I was, once again, being probed and prodded by dozen of nurses and staff. I was a bit worried. I tried to ask questions, but the nurse advised me to save all my questions for Dr. Chow. They assured me that everything was fine.

When Dr. Chow entered the room, I blurted, "I'm not due for another three weeks!"

"Calm down young lady. You're just fine. It's not unheard of to be a little early or even a little late when going into labor. Sometimes women even go into false labor. The thing is, it's very difficult to pinpoint the exact date you'll give birth, but we do the best we can. We take into consideration your last menstrual period and other factors. That's why it is very important for women to keep track of the exact dates of their cycles."

Dr. Chow didn't seem nervous at all, so I figured I had better calm down. Sonja's phone rang and she went into the hallway to answer it. While she was out, Stuart ran into the room.

"Are you okay? Is she okay doc?"

"She's just fine. Her water broke and I'm going to examine her to see how far dilated she is." The doctor left our room and Stuart held me so tight, I thought I was going to fall out from asphyxia.

"I can't breathe," I said.

"I'm sorry. I was so worried about you when Sonja called. I'm so glad she was there with you."

"Babe, I'm fine, calm down."

"Are you alright? Do you need anything?"

I looked at Stuart. "Why does it seem like *you're* the one having the baby?" We both chuckled at that one.

Sonja came back into the room. "Señor Charlie's flight leaves San Francisco in an hour and a half. He says he will be here as soon as he can."

Stuart and I thanked Sonja for being there.

"De nada. So now, I'll get out of your hair."

"No Sonja. I want you here when the baby is born. Okay? Aunt Sonja?" She smiled. "You're family, remember?"

"Si," she smiled.

Dr. Chow came back in with a nurse and asked if I wanted privacy or if it was okay if Sonja and Stuart stayed in the room. I advised him that I wanted them both there.

Dr. Chow instructed me to relax. I did. "Nine centimeters. You're almost ready to deliver this bundle of joy." He instructed the nurse to bring in the ultra sound machine so he could make sure the baby's heartbeat was healthy and get a better idea of how many pounds the baby was.

After he rubbed my belly with that cold gel, he scanned my stomach with the wand from the machine. Then he listened to the baby's heartbeat.

"Oh my. A strong and healthy heartbeat. And, I hate to tell you this Renee, but we're going to have to deliver this baby via Caesarean Section."

I looked at him, then at Stuart then back at him. "C-sa-wha?" I asked.

"Caesarean Section. C-Section. This baby looks to be well over ten pounds and that's too big for a vaginal birth."

He had the nurse take my blood pressure again. It was rising. He explained that it was better health wise for both the baby and me. After he gave me all the procedural propaganda, he had me sign forms authorizing the c-section and before I knew it, the nurse had slipped something in my IV and I was out.

I woke up groggy and out of it. The drugs the nurse had given me were starting to wear off. I looked around and saw Stuart standing next to the window in my room talking to someone on the phone. After a few minutes, I guessed it was Charlie. I was disappointed that Charlie couldn't have been here to witness the birth of his niece.

"Where is my baby?" I asked Stuart.

"Right here," a nurse said entering the room and handing me my newborn. "She's so beautiful. Congratulations on your little girl," she said.

"It's a girl?" I looked at Stuart with tears of joy. He beamed at me. I reached out for the nurse to put my baby in arms.

I held her tightly in my arms and beamed down at her with pride. God was truly amazing. She had one eye open and her little hands were balled into fists.

Stuart was also beaming with pride. "She came into the world with balled fist. Bad . . . just like her mama."

I held the baby close and snug. I didn't want to ever let her go. She made baby goo-goo noises. I joined in and the little angel gave me a smile.

Stuart filled me in on the details. She was ten pounds and nine ounces. She was twenty-two inches long and unlike Stuart or me, she was as white as a ghost.

"You sure this is our baby?" I asked Stuart jokingly.

"If it wasn't, it is now," he responded. We continue to adore the baby and talk about all the things we were going to do for her and how she would have a better life than either of us had.

"Where is Mr. Thatcher?" I asked Stuart.

"He should be on his way. That was him I was talking to on the phone. He had just landed at Lindberg Field. So he should be here shortly."

"Good. I want to wait until he gets here before we name her. You did say he could give the baby her middle name right?"

"I sure did. Just as long he doesn't name her Becky or Sue Ellen." We both laughed.

We heard a commotion in the hallway. Stuart went to the doorway to investigate. He turned around and looked at me with a shocked expression on his face. He put his head in hands and shook it.

"You're not going to believe this," he said.

"What?"

Stuart stood out of view of the doorway and just stared at me for a few seconds.

"*What?*" I asked anxiously. Right when I asked, a group of men and women entered the room with dozens of flowers, tons of teddy bears and other gifts.

"Oh my God. Where is Charlie? I know this can't be anyone but him."

After the last eight-foot panda came through the door, Charlie appeared. He kissed me on my forehead, but barely acknowledged me or anyone else for that matter. He quickly swept the baby from my arms.

"This is my little niece, my little angel. I am going to spoil you rotten. Yes I am. Yes I am," he said in baby talk.

Stuart, Sonja and I broke out in laughter. As usual, Charlie had done it big . . . *too* big if you ask me.

"You're going to get us thrown out of this hospital Chuck," I told him.

"And I'll sue the bajesus out of them too. Then my niece will have an even bigger trust fund than the one she already has." I rolled my eyes. He was too much, but I loved Charlie . . . we all did.

"So what did you name my angel?" he asked.

"We were waiting on you," Stuart answered.

"Why?"

"I told you Stuart said you could help name the baby," I answered.

"I didn't think you really *meant* it," he said. I rolled my eyes.

"So what do you suggest Chuck?" Stuart asked him.

"I like Violet because she is as beautiful as a flower. I thought you liked Justice," he said to Stuart.

"I do," Stuart answered. "So how are we going to make that work?"

"Violet Justice Humphries," I said.

"That doesn't sound right does it?" Stuart asked.

"Sounds good to me," I answered. "She's a prestigious flower." I guess that was explanation enough. We had picked out her name. Violet Justice Humphries. I wanted my child to have a name that was fit for royalty and heads of state. And here, she had both.

I was released from the hospital the next day and I continually thanked Sonja for the great job she had done with the nursery. The mint green worked out very well and now that everyone knew she was a girl, there were pink things galore. Violet received so much stuff, we had to store some of it and give away the rest.

Charlie informed me that he and Sonja would stay a few weeks to make sure, Stuart, the baby and I had everything we needed. This was my first child. I was going to take all the help I could get. Sonja made sure a room was prepared for Charlie. When he first bought this house, I thought it was ridiculous to have so many bedrooms, but now, they sure came in handy.

Chapter 18

A few months had passed, and I was so busy getting acclimated to being a new mother and taking care of Violet that it had been a while since I had called Barbara Jean to check up on her and to make sure that she was still taking her medication.

I dialed her number. I got a message that said the number I had reached was disconnected or no longer in service. I must have dialed the wrong number, so I dialed again. I got the same message. I dialed Susan's number.

"Hello?"

"Hi Susan. I just tried to call Barbara Jean but her phone is disconnected."

"I told you Lester was putting her in nursing home," she snapped.

"Why didn't you guys stop him from putting her in the nursing home?" I asked. She wanted to get snappy with me, but I was the daughter that lived over fifteen hundred miles away, while she and ten other brothers and sisters, a son, mother and other relatives lived within twenty miles of Barbara Jean.

"She's not *my* mother, she's *yours*," she said.

"True, but she *is* your sister. She is your mother's daughter. She is my brother's mother. None of you had a problem with her putting you in her will and her insurance policies as her beneficiaries, but you don't want to take care of her, what kind of crap is that?"

"You know Renee, I wish I could tell you what I really want to tell you, but it's not my place."

"Well guess what Susan? I already know. Jasmine told me and Barbara Jean confirmed it, so go to hell. What hospice care is my mother in?"

"Denver Hospice," she said before disconnecting the line.

I excused myself from the table and went into my office to search AOL for the Denver Hospice Care Center. When I found it, I dialed the number and asked the receptionist for Barbara Jean Jackson's nurse.

When the nurse answered, I explained to her who I was. She told me that Barbara Jean had been there for a few weeks, and now she wouldn't eat anything. I asked if I could talk to her and she put Barbara Jean on the phone.

"Hello," she said weakly.

"Hi Mom. How are you doing?"

"How you thank I'm doin'? I can't believe you let them put me in here."

"Mom, I tried to get you to come down here with me, but you didn't want to. I had already cleared everything with your doctor."

"I thought afta' I took you out my will, you didn't wanna help me."

"Do you really think I want anything from you? Do you really think that you have anything that I can't buy for myself? I don't want your money or anything else Barbara Jean. I've never asked you for anything. I have my own money—way more than you, I might add. So, I don't see why you thought that. I think you let those other folks tell you what they thought you'd believe and you did."

"Why Lesta' say you was gone leave me on the beach?"

"Why do you think he said it Mom? He's stole your money before and he's done it again. Do you really think I

161

would have been begging you to come down here if I didn't want to help you? We don't have the best of history, but you have nothing I want. I just want to see you get better so you can move on with your life."

"Why you leave in the first place?"

"Are you *serious?* I can't believe you would ask me a question like that. You were the reason I left. I know the cancer has affected your brain, but I know you know what you did." She became silent.

"Mom? Mama? Mother? Barbara *Jean!*" I shouted. She didn't respond to either. "I know you can hear me. I have to go check on my baby. By the way, you're a grandmother. I'll talk to you tomorrow." I heard her hang up the phone. This woman was going to be the death of me yet.

I was startled by Stuart standing in the doorway. I explained to him what had happened and that Lester had placed Barbara Jean in hospice care.

"I think that was the worst mistake they could have made. She's not going to do well in there. I know her, and if she stays there, her days are numbered.

"Come here," Stuart said as he motioned for me to come to him. I obliged his request. He took my hand and led me up the stairs to our bedroom.

He motioned for me to kneel down as he kneeled next to me. He prayed a powerful prayer as he squeezed my hands. I affirmed his prayers by saying amen and hallelujah. I knew Stuart could pray, but I had never heard him pray as fervently as he was now. He prayed long and hard.

After the prayer, he lifted me to my feet and held me for a while. "It's in God's hands now," he said.

✝   ✝   ✝

The next day, after I had fed Violet, I put her in her playpen and called the Hospice Care Center. Barbara Jean's nurse told me that Barbara Jean had stopped walking and that she would only use a wheelchair.

"How are you doing today Mother?" I asked her when she got on the phone.

"A'right."

"Are you eating?"

"Yea." I knew she was lying. Her nurse had already told me that she hadn't been eating lately.

"Did I tell you yesterday that you were a grandmother?"

"Yea. I'm too young to be a grandmother," she said. I laughed nervously. "Wha's her name?" she asked.

"Violet Justice Humphries," I answered proudly.

"White name huh?"

"A fitting name," I said. I knew she hadn't completely lost her faculties. She was still mean and evil as ever.

"Has anyone been to visit you?" I asked.

"No," she answered. That didn't surprise me. I don't know why I even asked.

After a minute, I could hear people in the background, but when I called her name, she didn't respond. Shortly thereafter, her nurse picked up the phone and explained that Barbara Jean laid the phone down and went back to her room. I thanked her and hung up. I felt defeated.

I looked back over at Violet, who was sitting in her playpen. She was wailing her hands and kicking her feet back and forth. She was looking at the mobile that was housed on the side of the pen, and responding to its movement and the music that came from it. I sang the words to her as I played with her kicking feet. She gaga'd and goo-goo'd as she scooted around the pen.

"I wanna be a Care Bear. Oh, it will be so great when I'm a Care Bear. Oh, I can hardly wait to be a Care Bear, and do the things Care Bears do."

Violet continued to gaga and goo-goo. I smiled at her and talked baby talk with her for a while. I picked her up and kissed her on her fat cheeks. She let out a loud burp. I patted her on her back for a few moments and before I knew it, she was sleeping.

† † †

Stuart and I had gotten tickets to the Old School Jam in the Gaslamp Quarter downtown. I was friends with one of the members of the musical group, Lakeside. When it came to music, I was definitely old school. The music that was being made today was trash in my opinion. In addition to Lakeside, The Barkays, Cameo and Confunkshun were appearing on stage.

I was surprised to see that even though I had just given birth to Violet just a few short months before, I was a little pudgy in the middle. I had been working out vigorously.

As usual, when we got downtown, parking was scarce. We finally found a space about three blocks away and walked to the event. Stuart and I walked past vendors selling goods and various types of foods. I bought a few little trinkets and Stuart saw a stuffed animal that he felt Violet just had to have. She didn't need it. She didn't need half the things she had.

Two hours later, no one had taken the stage. My patience began to wear thin. If I knew this would be the case, I would have chosen to stay home with my baby. I found Bill, my friend from Lakeside and he assured us that they would be taking the stage in less than twenty minutes. I assured him that if they weren't I would be leaving.

Stuart and I waited around a little longer. We decided to sample some of the international foods from a few of the vendors. When an hour had passed, I texted Bill to let know that we were leaving and I'd see him some other time.

When we got home, Violet was sound asleep. Sonja was in the garage painting and Charlie was in Stuart's office on his laptop. I took my shoes off and headed for Violet's nursery. She was sound asleep looking as angelic as ever. I kissed my fingers and pressed them to her cheek.

"I love you, little one," I whispered to her. She made me so happy and so proud to be a mother. I touched her little fingers, her little nose, her little toes and her round belly. She had a head full of dark hair that was starting to curl. She had on a Care Bear jumper. She was absolutely adorable. I stood there for a moment and watched her chest rise and fall. I smiled harder.

This was my daughter and I was responsible for making sure she had the very best in life and that she grew up with values and morals and was successful. It was my responsibility to mold her into the best person she could be. I was responsible for keeping her safe and teaching her the things she needed to know about life. I was sure she would develop into a fine young woman.

I went back downstairs and joined Stuart, Charlie and Sonja at the table in the kitchen. Sonja had set up a salad bar and we dove in.

As we were eating and discussing who would spoil Violet the most—and Charlie and Sonja's return trip to San Francisco, my cell phone rang. It was Susan. I looked at Stuart and took a deep breath.

"Hello?"

"Where have you been?" Susan yelled.

"Excuse me?"

"We've been trying to call you all night," she said.

"Who is *we*?"

"Me and Eddie. Where have you been?"

"None of your damn business. What do you want?"

"Barbara Jean is in the hospital!"

"What happened?"

"She's in a coma."

"I just talked to Barbara Jean earlier today. What are you talking about?"

Susan began to get a bit too mouthy for my tastes and I didn't have time to go round and about with her so I hung up on her and called the hospice.

The nurse explained to me that in addition to Barbara Jean not eating or walking, she had also stopped talking. She informed me that Barbara Jean had fallen into a coma and had been transported back to St. Joseph's hospital.

I called and talked to Barbara Jean's doctor. He confirmed that Barbara Jean was in a coma and advised that I get to Denver as soon as I could. I explained to him that I had just had a baby. He understood but stated he didn't expect Barbra Jean to make it much longer. I remembered just a little more than ten months ago, he had told us that Barbara Jean had about eleven months to live. It was almost eleven months. I knew I had to get to Denver, even if only to say goodbye.

I told Stuart and Charlie about Barbara Jean. I wasn't sure what type of reception I'd get when I told them I had to go back to Denver to see Barbara Jean one last time. To my surprise, Stuart was very receptive, Charlie on the other hand, was not.

"I'll make the arrangements now," Charlie offered. "We'll leave first thing in the morning."

"You and Stuart don't have to go. Sonja can help with Violet . . ." Before I could go on, Stuart interrupted me.

"Like hell. If you think I'm going to let you go down there by yourself, you're crazy. We're not going even going to discuss it. This is not a time for you to be by yourself *Mrs. Independent.*" He chuckled and so did I.

"I love you Mr. Humphries. Thank you."

"I love you too Mrs. Humphries," he said.

Charlie rolled his eyes at us both. "Can we finish eating before you two start?" I laughed and blew him a kiss. I love you too Chuck." Everyone got a laugh out of that one.

After dinner, I was emotionally and physically exhausted. I figured I had better take advantage of Violet's nap by taking one myself.

I called Sonja through the baby monitor to let her know that I would be napping and asked her to check in on Violet from time to time.

When I woke up, I checked in on Violet. She was still sound asleep. I wish I felt as peaceful as she looked at that moment.

I went downstairs and found Stuart and Charlie in his office having a chat. They both got quite when I walked in.

"Don't stop on my behalf," I said.

"How are you feeling?" Charlie asked me.

"Fine," I said defensively. I knew they were plotting, *what* I didn't know. They looked guilty. I looked at them both, shook my head and left the room.

I went into the kitchen and noticed that Sonja had made homemade croissants. They smelled so good and they tasted even better. I knew I shouldn't, but I ate two of them. I had to wash my guilt away somehow, so I went to the workout room to burn a few calories. I turned on the baby monitor so I could hear Violet.

I got on the stair climber and went at it. By the time I was done, I had burned eight hundred and twenty two calories. I felt a little better about eating those delicious croissants.

I checked on Violet once more. She was still sleep. I made sure she was dry and headed back downstairs. I surveyed the fridge and the cabinet in search of a Perrier. I found one in the bottom of the fridge.

Charlie and Stuart were still in Stuart's office scheming and plotting, so I decided to go upstairs and start packing. I only planned on staying in Denver for two weeks. Eventually, I had to get back to my own life. I packed a suitcase for me, one for Stuart and two for Violet. That was a shame, she was only a little baby and she had *two* suitcases. *Too* funny.

Chapter 19

After our plane landed, we rented a car and drove straight to the hospital. When we got there, the entire family—with the exception of Eddie, was standing around the nursing station. Instantly, I knew something was wrong.

I marched past everyone without speaking and entered the ICU bay where my mother was. I hugged Memah and looked at my mother. She had gained so much weight, her entire body was extremely bloated. I hardly recognized her. She had tubes in her nose and her mouth and IV needles in her arms. Keeping my composure at this time was not an option. I broke down in tears as I kissed my mother's hand. It felt so soft. I stared at her and found it hard not to cry. Stuart tried to comfort me, but nothing could comfort me at this point.

Here my mother lay, helpless, hanging onto every inch of her life. She was not responsive at all. It was evident that the only thing keeping her alive was the life support machine and the grace of God. In all that I had witnessed Barbara Jean endure in her lifetime, this was the hardest.

Dr. Abrams pulled me to the side and explained that her cancer had grown at a rapid pace and had caused her to have a seizure. He said there was nowhere for the tumor to go except through her vocal chords, otherwise it would explode. Then he dropped a bomb on me that would have me making one of the biggest decisions in my life.

"Since no one else wants to take on the responsibility, we need you to decide whether or not to take your mother off life support."

"Say what?" I asked.

"Here are the options. If we leave her on life support, the tumor will either come through her throat or, it will simply explode." The thought made me nauseous. Dr. Abrams continued, "On the other hand, we can take her off life support and let her breathe on her own and see how it goes."

I leaned against Stuart so that I would not fall. How could he ask me to make that decision?

"When do I have to make this decision?" I asked him.

"Now," he responded. "It's really a matter of if you want your mother to die with dignity or not. Taking her off life support and letting nature take its course, will be far more dignified then having the tumor explode."

"But I'm not her power of attorney." I tried another approach. I pointed to Lester. "He is."

"He, nor anyone else in the family will make the call, so as her daughter, I need you to make the call."

"You bastard!" I yelled towards Lester. "You can take her money but not make the decision she left you to make?"

Lester came towards me but Stuart stepped in front of me. "I dare you," he told Lester. Lester stood back. Stuart turned back to me.

"Baby, just make the decision you think is best, so we can leave this trash where it is and get on with our lives."

"*Trash?*" Susan said.

"Shut up Susan! *Now* you want to speak up? Just shut the hell up," I said. I paced back and forth in front of the nurses desk for a moment and then returned to Barbara Jean's side.

I studied her and wondered what she would have wanted. We had talked about her will and other business a long time ago. When she realized I wasn't going to be her puppet, she told me that she would be taking me off her will and adding Lester as her power of attorney and beneficiary. I assured her that I didn't want anything from her, but also warned her that Lester and the rest of the family wrote her off for dead before, they wouldn't hesitate to do it again. But she was so angry that she could no longer control me, she didn't give it a second thought.

I held her lifeless hand and prayed to the only person I knew could give me an answer. Stuart came up behind me and put his hands on my shoulders. "Put it in God's hands," he whispered. I asked him to have the doctor come in so I could give him the answer that God had given me and that Stuart had confirmed.

The nursing staff, under the direction of Barbara Jean's doctors removed her tubes. I guess I expected her to stop breathing as soon as the tubes were removed. Much to my relief she continued breathing.

I arranged to have a reclining chair placed next to Barbara Jean's bed. I was going to stay until she came out of her coma or until she took her last breath. I demanded that everyone else left, including Stuart. Everyone else was happy to leave, however, Stuart said he would stay in the waiting room with Charlie, Violet and Sonja, but refused to leave me there by myself.

I kept a close eye on my mother. If I thought I could fit in the bed, I would have slept in it with her.

Throughout the night, I read passages from Psalms, Proverbs, Deuteronomy and Isaiah.

Be strong and courageous. Do not fear or be in dread of them, for it is the LORD your God who goes with you. He will not leave you or forsake you.

Fear not, for I am with you; be not dismayed, for I am your God; I will strengthen you, I will help you, I will uphold you with my righteous right hand.

So we do not lose heart. Though our outer self is wasting away, our inner self is being renewed day by day. For this light momentary affliction is preparing for us an eternal weight of glory beyond all comparison, as we look not to the things that are seen but to the things that are unseen. For the things that are seen are transient, but the things that are unseen are eternal.

The LORD is a stronghold for the oppressed, a stronghold in times of trouble. And those who know your name put their trust in you, for you, O LORD, have not forsaken those who seek you.

I will lift up mine eyes unto the hills, from whence cometh my help.

After a while of reciting the verses, I felt my mother squeeze my hand. "I'm here Mother," I said. *"You're* not supposed to be here. We have some unfinished business to tend to." She moved her leg, then her head. Eventually, her eyes opened as she looked at me for a few seconds and then . . . she drifted away.

"You need to wake up. I don't' like the way they're talking," I told her. *No response.*

"I know you can hear me, wake up!" I yelled. She moved her left leg and squeezed my hand. "That's right," I said with joy.

All of a sudden, the monitor she was hooked to made a loud beeping sound. I panicked. The nurse came in and explained to me that the annoying sound only meant that Barbara Jean was responding to pain. She shot more morphine through her IV. After a while, she was unresponsive . . . again.

I continued to read bible verses until I could no longer recognize the words on the page. I eventually fell asleep.

I was awakened by footsteps stirring in the room. It was my uncle Fred, his wife, and their daughter. I stood over Barbara Jean to see if there were any changes in her vitals. Her eyelids were moving. I thought she might have been dreaming, until I realized that she was having another seizure. I panicked once more and let out a loud scream.

A nurse rushed into the room and proceeded to stabilize her. She injected more morphine into the IV. Barbara Jean's movement subdued.

After my uncle and his family left, I sat in my chair, said a prayer and read more bible verses to Barbara Jean. I kept an eye on her monitor and noticed that her stats were actually improving. I looked at her and smiled. There was one thing I could not deny—I got my fight from my mother. And she was indeed . . . fighting.

For a quick moment, I thought that perhaps we could start over and build our mother-daughter relationship. I rubbed her feet and then squeezed her hand. Her eyes were rolling under her eyelids. I knew she knew I was there and without words, she certainly wanted the same thing that I wanted.

"Good morning," I said to her. This was the most movement I had seen from her in the past few hours. I folded the blanket I had used to cover myself and rubbed her feet once more. There was more movement. I was optimistic. The readings on her monitor had improved in a matter of minutes and this gave me more hope and confidence that she was going to beat this.

I looked up and saw Stuart standing in the doorway. "How's she doing?" he asked.

"Actually, she's getting a lot better. Her vitals are improving and she's shown movement in her eyes, her hands *and* her feet."

"That's a blessing," Stuart said with enthusiasm. We held a long embrace. I took a deep breath and then let out a sigh of relief.

"How's my angel?" I asked him, shifting my focus to Violet.

"Being spoiled by her aunt and God father as usual. I sent them back to the hotel. I don't want Violet catching any germs." I smiled and asked him to stay in the room while I took a shower.

I gathered my clothes and hygiene products and jumped into the shower. My mind began to wander. Now that Barbara Jean was recovering, what was I going to do? I know I didn't want to stay in Denver any longer than I had to and I knew Stuart wasn't going to like that idea either. I had to find some way to convince Barbara Jean to move to San Diego with us . . . something else I knew Stuart wasn't going to be too happy about.

I was sure that my mother would love San Diego if she just gave it a chance. I would have to prepare one of the spare bedrooms downstairs for her so she wouldn't have to struggle with the stairs. That wouldn't be a problem. I'd have to hire a nurse for her. That wouldn't be a problem either. Her health care provider was Kaiser Permanente and they just happened to have offices in San Diego. I had already gotten approval from her doctor to relocate her.

My thoughts were interrupted by Stuart's panicky voice. My heart began to race.

"Babe!" he said. "I think you may want to come out here." I shouted from the shower and asked him what the problem was.

"Now! Just put on a towel," was all he said.

The strain in his voice made my heart pump faster. I wrapped a white hospital towel around my wet torso and opened the bathroom door. Two nurses were standing at the foot of my mother's bed. I couldn't see my mother because Stuart was standing by her side. I looked at the two nurses and the look on their faces, told me what I had feared. I brushed past Stuart and looked at my mother's face then to her heart monitor.

I watched her heart rate drop. *81 . . . 77 . . . 63 . . . 52 . . . 41 . . . 38 . . . 33 . . . 27 . . . 23 . . . 17 . . . 10 . . . 9 . . . 6 . . . 2 . . .*

The monitor beeped as it flat lined. I burst into tears. There was no attempt to revive her. We all knew the inevitable was happening. Barbara Jean had passed away before our very eyes. I looked at the clock on the wall—it was 8:36 a.m.

A small stream of tears rolled down my face. I wiped them away before they could reach my cheek. Confusion set in. Barbara Jean had just died and I wasn't throwing myself around in a dramatic tirade. I tried crying harder, but it didn't work.

Suddenly I was jolted back. Nothing had physically touched me, yet some unknown source had moved me. My heart nearly leaped out of my chest when I saw what looked like a demon adorned in black tattered cloth, run from the left side of my mother's bed. After it stopped for a moment to glare at me in disdain, it disappeared into dissolution.

Then another figure shot from the right side of Barbara Jean's head as another rose from the top of her bed. This super natural, out of body experience went on for a few minutes as the smoky ghost-like figures ran in directions opposite of my mother's body—thirty-two in all. I collapsed onto the floor.

When I came to, there were nurses surrounding me causing a ruckus. Stuart was trying to get to me, but they kept telling him to stand back. I don't know how long I was out, but my attention was drawn to my brother. He had arrived when I was out cold. I could see him out the corner of my eye, sitting on the side of Barbara Jean's bed bawling like a baby.

A white light quickly flashed before my eyes and disappeared. Suddenly a strange sense of peace came over me as I tried to figure out what had just happened. Thirty-two demons. I had turned thirty-two just a few weeks earlier. My revelation, my freedom . . . Is that what it meant? I was free . . . or was I? Was I free of Barbara Jean's draining mental hold? Free from thirty-two years of bondage? Free to finally find myself and live for me? If so, how? I had an epiphany—her stronghold is what kept me going. I wasn't sure if I knew how to survive without her.

I shook the countless fingers, hands and medical instruments from my personal space as I lifted myself from the floor and came to my brother's aide. I certainly couldn't say *don't cry*. There was *some* sense of sadness on my part, but for him, he was her favorite. For he had suffered a greater loss than I had. Now, he had to grow up. I didn't know what he was going to do without her. Without her, we he was lost.

I put my arms around his shoulders and lay my head on his back as he laid *his* head on my mother's chest. Her cold, clammy skin soaked up his tears. Stuart stood back and gave us space.

Time of death?" I heard a voice ask from somewhere in the room.

"8:36," I heard another say. 8:36. 8:36. 8:36. Time of death 8:36. She *expired* at 8:36, but I was sure she had died *long* ago. I suspected she had died that awful day back in 1968, when her father *and* her mother had taken her innocence. No, not 8:36. 1968 was when she died.

I lifted myself from my brother. I studied his attachment to my mother. I knew it would take the Jaws of Life to remove him from her now. Me, I had to be the voice of reason, the responsible one. There were funeral arrangements to be made. In spite of all she had done, she deserved a decent burial. Yes, in spite of. Stuart and I left the room as I started making the necessary calls.

"She's gone," I told my grandmother when she answered the phone. Her response wasn't surprising. It was rather nonchalant. I gathered it was because *her* hell, the hell she had lived all these years, her accessory to the rape of her oldest daughter had finally come to and end. The guilt that stared her in the face for fifty-two years had come to the end of its sentence.

I disconnected the line. I refused to call anyone else. I knew that she would spread the word. Soon the very hospital room where I had just reclaimed my freedom would be filled with spectators who would come to pay homage to the late great Barbara Jean Matthews.

Lester walked in first. He began barking orders to the nurse to do this to do that. As other family members and friends arrived, he barked orders to them. *Now* he wanted make decisions. He punked out and forced me to choose whether to leave or take my mother of life support. How convenient. He could dictate how my mother's money would be spent, but he didn't want the responsibility or have the balls to end her life. No, he didn't want that on his conscious . . . what little he preserved.

† † †

"She has about three life insurance policies that I know of," I said back at my grandmother's apartment.

"She only had two," Lester interjected.

"She had three," I defended my position. "She showed them to me."

"She had two," he said again.

"She had three," I said curtly. "You may only plan to use two and use the other one, the one that you think no one knows about for yourself, but she had three." I rolled my eyes and walked away from him. I stood by Stuart and whispered in his ear for him to call Charlie. He was one step ahead of me. He stepped outside to make the call. I knew Barbara Jean had at least three insurance policies and there was probably another. I knew Charlie could find out.

Stuart came back in after talking to Charlie. I listened as the rest of the family discussed what they were going to do with Barbara Jean's money, what they were going to for the funeral. I was in disbelief.

About an hour later, the text alert chimed on Stuart's cell phone. Charlie had found the information we needed him to find. I read the text to everyone in the room.

"Barbara Jean had a total of six life insurance policies totaling seven hundred and fifty thousand dollars. And none of you sons of bitches better ask me for one red cent to help toward this funeral. I know you all have her money mapped out. But you damn well better make sure she gets a proper burial." With that, Stuart and I left Memah's apartment and headed to our hotel room across town.

Four brothers, five sisters, a mother, a son and host of other family and friends and *I* was the one responsible for cleaning my mother's apartment. They took it upon themselves to deal with everything that had to do with her money, while leaving me with the responsibility of the cleanup work.

I cursed my mother in my mind for changing that power of attorney and her beneficiary documents at the last minute. I wanted nothing from my mother, but just like in times past, I knew she was going to be taken advantage of, even in her death.

I was given the key to her apartment, but not before my aunts had made a beehive to get what they wanted first, leaving Eddie and me with what was left. I was feeling overwhelmed.

"I'm so glad you came babe," I told Stuart. "I don't think I could have done this without you."

"There was no way I was going to let you come alone. You will get through this. After the funeral, we will head back to San Diego and you'll never have to see this God awful place again." I knew Stuart didn't mean Denver, but rather my family, or poor excuse of one.

"Are you hungry?" Stuart asked me.

"Yes, actually, I am."

"Let's go out for a bite," he suggested. I didn't want to go out, so he decided he'd take me back to the hotel to see Violet and we'd eat there.

After Stuart left to pick up Italian, I made sure Violet was sleeping. Charlie was in one of the conference rooms conducting business, while Sonja wrote in her journal. I took a hot shower and sat on the sofa. I put my feet up on the coffee table, put my head back and closed my eyes. Another chapter of my life was closed, but I was still finding it hard to deal with the reality that Barbara Jean was gone.

My thoughts were interrupted by Stuart's passkey at the door. The delightful aroma of Italian food tickled my nostrils. Stuart unpacked the food and sat it on the table in the tiny kitchenette.

"Looks good. Smells good," I said. I closed my eyes and took in a long deep breath, inhaling the food. The smell must have wakened Violet, because her little head was bouncing on the bed as she let out a light wail. I picked her up and began baby talk with her. I asked Stuart to text Charlie to let him know that the food had arrived.

"So what's next on your agenda?" Stuart asked after sending the text.

"Well," I took a bite of food. "I have to call the movers, pack up Barbara Jean's things and clean her apartment."

"What are you going to do with her things?" he asked.

"Well I really have no choice but to ship them to California."

"Like *we* need more things. We don't have room. Where are we going to put everything? And why can't your brother take them?"

"And put them where?" I asked. I looked up at Stuart. "He says he has no where to put them. Besides, he skips from woman to woman. He doesn't know where he'll sleep on any given night. And her sisters and brothers have taken so much from her already."

My cell phone rang. I looked at the caller ID. It was Lester. I sent the call straight to voice mail. Barbara Jean was gone so there was no urgency at least not on my part.

"So what movie did you get?" I asked focusing completely on Stuart.

"When a Man Loves A Woman, Die Hard 2 and Me, Myself, and Irene." I laughed. Stuart could be so corny—almost as corny as Charlie.

We spent the duration of the evening eating and watching movies. I fell asleep on Stuart's chest half way through Me, Myself and Irene. The movie was funny but I was exhausted. When I woke up, he was watching ESPN, Charlie was sleep on the sofa, with drool running from the side of his mouth. Sonja and Violet lay sound asleep on one of the double beds.

"Hey sleepyhead," Stuart said.

"What time is it?" I asked.

"Two-twenty."

"In the morning?"

"Yes," he replied I hadn't planned on sleeping that long. I headed to the bathroom to take a shower. I let the water run down my back as I tried to wash away the days dirt and grime. I wanted this to all be over so I could get back to San Diego and my life. I had to stay in this hellhole for five more days.

Chapter 20

Susan and Memah drove in the limo with Stuart, Charlie, Violet, Sonja and I. We were to meet a Lester's house and proceed to the church from there. When we arrived at Lester's home, there were only a few cars and a handful of people standing out in the front yard. Soon after, more and more cars arrived, as more and more bodies congregated on the front lawn. I refused to go inside Lester's house and I really didn't want mingle, so I stayed in the limo.

When the cars from the funeral home arrived, the immediate family was placed in selected limos and town cars. I chose to stay in the limo that Charlie had gotten for us.

When we arrived at the church, several people were packing the pews inside. The family was ushered in and seated up front. It was obvious by the number of people there, that Barbara Jean was a very popular person. There had to be at least five hundred in attendance. The choir from her church sat in the choir stand, dressed in red and black robes. Her former pastor sat in the pulpit.

After being seated, my attention focused on the closed coffin in front of me. It was adorned with a bouquet of soft peach and mauve roses.

I tried to divert my attention elsewhere, but failed in doing so. The thought of Barbara Jean, my mother, lying inside that coffin with no life left inside her, seemed so unreal to me. I forced myself not to shed a tear. I wanted to be strong. I had to be strong for my brother, who was falling apart at the seams. I comforted him as he cried—and kept my composure.

The choir sang a few selections. Various ministers said a few words and turned the service into church service.

Towards the end of the ceremony, anyone who wanted to pay a few words of acknowledgment or condolence was able to do so.

I listened to everyone as they expressed how much they missed my mother and how close they were to her. Some said she was like a second mother, others said she taught them how to be ladies. This struck a nerve because these were all the things I wanted my mother to be to me, but she never was. It wasn't until my god sister, Shyanne broke into tears, that I thought I would surely lose my mind. I could no longer hold back my tears. Stuart consoled me.

After the pastor read Barbara Jean's eulogy, the funeral directors positioned themselves in front of her coffin for the viewing. I stared at her corpse as if I was staring straight through her. I was still trying to deal with the fact that the corpse in the casket was really my mother. It didn't look like her to me. More like a waxed version of her. She looked two times her weight, her skin was ash grey and appeared to be melting. Her fingers were sunk in as if she had no flesh and bone inside.

Denial hit me. This was not my mother laying here. I was having a nightmare and eventually I'd wake up, call her and tell her all the things I wanted to, should have, but never did.

It was my turn to say a few words. I had written them down. I had to put on a good face. I couldn't very well go up there in front of all these people and tell them what a horrible mother she was. I couldn't tell them that she didn't teach me the things she should have. And I certainly couldn't tell them she failed at her motherly duties and promises to protect me. No, I would make the words as kind as I possibly could. Once I did, I was free to go home and be with my family, make my own memories and be held to the same standards, as a mother, that Barbara Jean should have.

I began to read:

Until we meet again. When Barbara Jean was first diagnosed with cancer, I was given a scripture; no weapon formed against me shall prosper. Selfishly I thought that the scripture pertained to my life. Six months later a second verse was revealed to me; weeping may endure for a night, but joy comes in the morning. Again, selfishly I thought the Lord was trying to prepare me for the happenings in my life. This was revealed to me over and over in several forms.

I recalled the night before my mother's journey ended, reciting to her that same scripture. It was not until I saw her breathe her last breath that I realized that this revelation was not for me at all, but in fact a message for her. Several people had told me that they were interceding and praying, knowing if she just made it through the night, she would be all right. The night before she passed, I had slept no more than four feet from her hospital bed. I checked on her and she was holding her own. The following morning, I checked on her and she was still holding her own. I may never know why she chose to wait until I got in the shower to take her journey home. But somehow, things began to become clearer to me.

I think now, of all the good times and smile because in the midst of my mother's journey, she taught me love, grace, style tenacity and how important it is to be strong for your children. She also taught me patience and endurance. When I look in the mirror, I see my mother looking back at me. I had no idea her favorite bible verses were the same as mine. My mother touched several lives—many of you that are here today. Whether it was a smile, a touch, a hug, advice, or an opinion, her service or simply her presence. Either way she touched us all in a way that will always be remembered. So, those of you that are weeping today, remember in my mother's fifty two years of God given life, she served her intended purpose. Know that her service was pleasing in the Lord's sight, therefore I know Heaven is her home, her final destination. Mama, we want you to know, we will always love and remember you. Until we meet again.

After I read those words, I wondered why I had written them. I meant none of them. They were actually all the things that I thought she should have been. The fact was I was afraid of my mother all my life. When it came to learning about this cold hard and cruel world, I learned by trial and error. I knew there were two things that I would always remember about Barbara Jean. One was how she never showed her children love and had it not been for Jasmine, I would have gone through life with unfinished business.

Eddie nervously took the microphone and tried to speak. Nothing came from his mouth. He tried again, still nothing came out. I rubbed his back and told him if he'd rather not say anything, he didn't have to.

"I just want to thank you all for coming out, and for loving my mother. She is smiling down on all of us right now," was all he said, before we took our places on the front pew.

During the viewing of Barbara Jean's body, her friends came around, shook our hands, and gave a smile, a glance or a hug as they viewed her body and returned to their seats.

Afterwards, the immediate family was allowed to view the body. I did not want to go at first. I didn't want to see her laying there. I didn't want to lose it. I had to be strong and I knew if I saw her lifeless body, I would look all control. I felt cheated.

I couldn't let them close the casket without as much as a goodbye, so I walked over to the beautiful bouquet of roses that were on the top and picked out one single peach rose and lay it on her chest. My hand shook tremendously, tears started to form, but I had to be strong. Eddie was counting on me.

After the last family member was done viewing the body, the casket was closed and the ushers carried it out to the waiting hearse. The family marched in unison behind them.

Once more, I found myself inside the same limousine trying to hold back tears. I couldn't let these people see me break down, or they will think I am weak and try to take advantage of me, I thought.

The funeral processional led us across town to Fairmount Cemetery, where my mother was to be laid to rest. I observed the various headstones and mausoleums as we drove by, wishing that one could have been afforded by Barbara Jean.

We all resided under a tarp near Barbara Jean's casket, by the plot where she was to be buried. Her pastor said a few words and then offered flowers to be taken from atop the casket before they lowered her corpse into the ground. I thought back to when Paw was put into the ground as I tried to jump into the plot with him. For some reason, this here was Barbara Jean, my mother, and I didn't feel the same way.

I started feeling guilty for a moment—that I wasn't as emotional as others thought I should have been. After pondering for a few moments, I decided, this time, I wasn't going to stay and watch the casket being lowered into the ground. I joined the rest of the family back at Lester's church for dinner. The fixings included turkey and dressing, ham, potato salad and peach cobbler.

That night after the funeral, I decided I would stay at Barbara Jean's apartment and pack the last bit of her belongings to take back to San Diego with me. The night was a hard one for me. I found myself getting up in the middle of the night packing and trying to take my mind off of her. The truth was, I was scared.

Stuart comforted me and we talked for what seemed like hours as I packed Barbara Jean's things. Most of it, I had decided to give away. I had no need for it and her sisters had taken what they wanted. There were a few collectible and antiques that I'd decided to save. In spite of, I felt that every family should have heirlooms that are passed from generation to generation. I had received nothing from Barbara Jean or Rosie for that matter. I decided to break that generational curse and pass something on to my daughter that she could pass on to hers.

The next morning, the movers arrived and loaded up Barbara Jean's china cabinet, expensive paintings, and all the things I had decided to take with me back to San Diego. I had called Eddie and asked if he wanted the things but he was in no position to take them. I would put them in storage—for how long, I had no idea.

Stuart made sure all the trash had been emptied while I made sure everything was clean and gave it a once over. Barbara Jean's landlord had told me if we had stayed a few days later, she would charge me for the extra three days that Barbara Jean's things remained in the apartment.

Like hell you will.

Barbara Jean had lived in "The Lakes" for over thirteen years and they had the nerve to be worried about three extra days of rent . . . and from a dead woman. I laid the keys on the counter and looked around the apartment. Another chapter had ended. I took a deep breath and shut the door behind me.

One year later . . .

Chapter 21

I woke up in a cold sweat. Déjà vu had engulfed me as I remembered that less than two years ago, I was at this very same place. Today, I would be walking down the aisle once more with Stuart. The nightmares that I had been having had subsided until now. This time, when I walked down the aisle to meet Stuart at the altar, guests were laughing and pointing at me. When Stuart raised my veil, it was Barbara jean instead of me.

Even though she had been dead for over a year, Barbara Jean still found a way to invade my spirit. Despite all I had done for her during her sickness, she had cursed me.

"I'm gone make sho' you ain't neva happy," she had told me. I was determined not to let her have that type of control over my life.

I had set the timer on the coffee pot the night before and now I could smell the aroma of the French roasted beans filling the house.

I went down to the kitchen and poured myself a cup of the murky brown heaven. I retreated to the great room and flipped on the television. A reporter on CNN was talking about 9/11 theories and leaks of President Bush's plan to enter into war with Iraq. I switched the channel. The last thing I needed was to hear about war or rumors of war on my wedding day.

I channel surfed for a few moments before I decided to park on a Jazz music channel. I switched over to the surround sound, turned up the volume and headed back upstairs.

As I ascended the staircase, I heard the phone ring. I knew it was either Stuart or Charlie.

"Well good morning beautiful," Stuart said when I answered.

"Well good morning to you, too, handsome." I smiled on the inside. Stuart and I agreed that he would stay at a hotel the weekend of the wedding and our little angel would stay with her Uncle Charlie—who I was sure was spoiling her at that very moment.

"How is my queen this morning?" Stuart asked me.

"Doing great, my king." I didn't want to concern Stuart with the nightmare I had experienced a few hours earlier so I didn't mention it.

"So, do you still want to be Mrs. Stuart Humphries?"

"I dunno," I teased.

"You're not going to leave me at the altar are you?"

"I might," I said sarcastically. We both laughed.

"Have you talked to Sunshine this morning?" I asked him. Sunshine was the many nicknames we had given to Violet—actually, it was the name Charlie had given her.

"As a matter of fact, I just did. I know you're not surprised that she has Chuck wrapped around her little finger."

"I know, but you know that's Charlie's fault. Now, Violet can experience what I have all these years." We both laughed because Charlie had been protective of me since day one.

"Well baby, I will see you when you walk down the aisle. Don't be late," he said before ending our conversation.

"I won't," I said.

"I love you."

"I love you too," I said before hanging up the phone.

I sat on my chaise for a moment and basked in the thought of finally becoming Mrs. Stuart Humphries. My next call was to my angel.

"Mommy!" she shrieked when she answered Charlie's phone.

"Heyyy Pumpkin. Are you behaving?" I asked.

"Yes ma'am," she giggled. It's funny, I had never seen myself having children but when Violet was born, I was overcome with joy. From that point on, she was the most important thing in my life. She had taught me so much and I was determined to show her how much she was loved each and every day.

She told me, or tried at least, everything she and Uncle Charlie had done the day before. Even though she was nearly two, Violet was smart and too clever for her own good. She knew her ABCs, how to count to one-hundred and even knew her colors in English *and* Spanish. Her vocabulary and intelligence far exceeded that of a two-year-old.

"I bet you are going to be beautiful in your dress today." I told her.

"Flowers on the ground!" she said with excitement.

"Just like we practiced."

"Love you mommy!"

"Love you too, Pump—," I guess my little girl had other things to do because before I could finish my sentence, Charlie was on the phone.

"Good morning Luv."

"Good morning Charlie. Has she sent you into bankruptcy yet?"

"You know it," he responded. We both laughed. When we had returned from Denver, Charlie decided he wanted to be closer to Violet, so he purchased an expensive condo in Mission Valley. We both knew that it was *Violet's* house and she only allowed Charlie to stay there—since *she* couldn't pay the mortgage.

"So today's the big day . . . again." I really wished he wouldn't have said that. The last thing I needed to do was think about the last time I had walked down the aisle.

"So you're okay with getting her ready?" I asked, trying to change the subject.

"I think I'm perfectly capable." We both knew that he wouldn't be the one making sure Violet was dressed and ready. I was sure Sonja would be the one primping Violet for the wedding.

"Are you sure you're going to be able to handle her during our honeymoon?"

"Hey, my god niece practically owns the place. She's so funny. I remember when she first visited. She *told* me, not asked me, but *told* me, which room was going to be hers. And I'll be darned if she wouldn't let me go into *her* bathroom." Again, we both chuckled. That sounded like my baby.

"I knew at that moment who was *really* in charge," Charlie added. I was impressed at how Charlie and Violet had taken to each other. Charlie never had children. He *couldn't* have any. He revealed his inability to have children during the only drunken binge I had ever witnessed. To this date, he doesn't remember telling me, and that's a secret I'll take to my grave.

We talked a few more moments, then I asked him to put Violet back on the line.

"Tuttle, mommy," she said once she got back on the phone.

"What?" I asked.

"Unk-el got me tut-el," she said. I rolled my eyes. There was no telling what *other* wishes Charlie had granted that child of mine.

"I'm going to see you later on my love. Mommy loves you."

"Love you mommy. Tut-el!" she shrieked, and then the line went dead. I chuckled to myself. I knew one thing, that turtle would stay at Uncle Charlie's house because there would be no way it would step foot in mine. I sighed. A turtle—my child was so fearless.

I showered, threw on a pair of faded jeans, black four-inch boots and a tan sweater and headed to my hair appointment.

"Girl, what have I told you about using rubber bands in your hair?" Shena asked me when I walked into her shop in Mission Valley. She had started out at a shop on University Avenue in North Park, but her high-end clientele afforded her a new shop on Fraze Road. It was the best choice she could have made, because anyone wanting to have their hair styled by 'Shena hair extraordinaire' had to be added to a three month waiting list.

"Now you know, with Violet in the house, I can't keep up with my scrunchies."

"How is that little poo butt doing?" she asked once I stopped laughing.

"She's doing well. She's with her Uncle Charlie right now."

Shena eyed me strangely. "Sometimes I have to remember whose child she is. Are you sure she isn't Charlie's baby?"

I rolled my eyes. "You need to stop." She wasn't the first person to question Violet's paternity. Violet was slightly lighter than Stuart and I, and had a good grade of hair . . . nappy, nonetheless. But, I was positive Violet was Stuart's. Charlie and I had stopped being intimate when Stuart and I started dating. And even though a DNA test wasn't necessary, after the hell we went through with Barbara Jean, we cleared up any doubts about it.

"Cut it all off," I said, stopping Shena before she could start.

"Are you serious?"

"Yes, *very.*" Even though I wore weaves on a regular basis, I had let my hair grow long, but I was ready for a change.

Shena stood behind me with one hand on her hip, looking at me through the mirror as if I had lost my mind. "Define short."

"Halle Berry short."

"Everybody wants to look like Halle Berry, but everybody *can't* look like Halle Berry."

"You know what I mean. I want my hair that short and styled similar to hers."

"Are you serious?"

"Dead."

Shena hesitated for a moment. "Okay," she finally said and then let out a deep sigh. She sharpened her sheers and worked her beauty magic on my crown and glory.

About an hour later, my long hair was transformed into a short, sexy masterpiece. I looked in the mirror in awe as I patted the sides and the back of my head. I looked pretty darn good with short hair.

"Girl, you did a magnificent job."

"Stuart's going to kill you, you know that right?"

"He'll be alright." I didn't even consider what Stuart might think. Oh well, he was going to have to get used to it. I gave Shena an even bigger tip than usual and told her I'd see her at the wedding later on that day.

I headed to the nail shop to get a manicure and a pedicure. Afterwards, I would head back home to relax for a few moments. Angie would help me get ready for my big day.

Charlie had assigned a car to pick me up so I didn't have too much to worry about.

When I got home, I sat in the oversized chair that sat in the great room. What I really wanted to do was take a nap, but I didn't' want to ruin my new hairstyle.

"Do you want something to eat?" Angie asked me.

"Sure, whatcha' got?"

"Mixed fruit and mineral water."

"Sounds good to me. Just as long as you don't give me any strawberries."

I relaxed for a few more moments before I decided to take a long hot bath and get ready for the wedding. I submerged myself into the hot sudsy water but made sure I didn't get my hair wet. The warm suds were a welcome tranquility. The further I sank into the oversized jetted garden tub, the more I drifted . . .

Drifting . . .

Drifting . . .

Drifting . . .

"I don't' know Nae, there were rumors that her father had raped her," Stuart had said.

Drifting . . .

Drifting . . .

"Why do you treat me the way you do?" I had asked Barbara Jean.

"I treat you tha same way my mama treated me," she said.

At the time, I couldn't imagine Memah treating Barbara Jean the way she had said. However, I had to really think about it. Barbara Jean, Eddie and I were treated differently than the rest of the family. Actually, we were the black sheep of the family. That was highly evident around Christmas time. Our cousins would receive a bounty of gifts, while Eddie and I were lucky enough to get a ninety-nine cent coloring book—minus the ninety-nine cent crayons.

Barbara Jean and Memah used to get into heated conversations about what the other had. Barbara Jean said that Memah resented her because she wanted to be like her. Memah had to follow her to Colorado. Whenever Barbara Jean would buy a piece of furniture, Memah would buy the same piece, but in a different color. I remembered once when Barbara Jean and Memah showed up to a family reunion celebration in the exact, same dress—it turned out to be a fiasco.

I often thought that since Memah and the rest of the family mistreated us, that Barbara Jean would treat Eddie and I much better. Then I remembered, I tried to remember, but couldn't. Barbara Jean had never told us that she loved us . . . *never*.

Hal had scolded her several times for never telling us that she loved us. I had always tried to figure out Barbara Jean's make-up, to no avail. Now that I thought about it, it all made more and more sense. Paw and I had a deep connection and I could never put my finger on it.

The knock on the door brought me out of deep thought. One day, I would have to call my aunt Jasmine and formally thank her for finally giving me the answers that I had searched for my entire life. If she had not told me the truth, both Barbara Jean and Memah would have taken that family secret to their graves.

Thank God, I had closure and I could heal and give myself to Stuart and Violet completely. I knew that I had to be the one to break the cycle and *that* I would. I couldn't imagine myself not loving my little girl and I knew I would seriously hurt *anyone* that tried to harm her.

"You need to wrap it up in there lady," Angie said from the other side of the door. "We need to get this show on the road."

I said a quick prayer and thanked God for bringing me this far. I didn't yet understand the path he had brought me, but I thanked him anyway, because I knew things could have gone much different.

I dried off and lathered myself with Sesame Oil. One of the things I loved about San Diego was the fact that it took little effort to moisturize my skin. When I lived in Denver, I had to use a heavy moisturizer, and *often*.

Unlike, my last trip down the aisle, I was going to be lenient on my make-up. In fact, nothing about this weeding was going to be as grand as the last. Bishop Trotter was going to marry us at *The Park*, and as opposed to hundreds of guest, we only invited a handful of family and friends. Charlie had protested, but this time I put my foot down.

I slipped my sundress on over my undergarments, made sure my dress and other necessities were in the limo, and then Angie and I were off to the church. I lowered the window and allowed the chilly fall air to creep in.

Chapter 22

The weather was overcast with spotty drizzle. I was glad we chose to have the wedding inside instead of outside. I just wished that there was a bit of sun. The weather was fit for a funeral and not a wedding. I figured I'd marry Stuart in the middle of a hurricane, so it really didn't matter.

Catering trucks and other industrial vehicles were parked in front of *The Park* when we arrived. Several service workers were preparing for the wedding. As I entered the church, I stopped for a moment and looked around. I got the eeriest feeling and it gave me goose bumps—it was as if I was having a bout of vertigo. I shooed the uncanny feeling off. Nothing was going to ruin this day for me. Barbara Jean was dead so I was sure I was overreacting. I proceeded into the church and downstairs. There was no sign of Stuart, Violet or Charlie.

I dialed Stuart's number first.

"Hey baby. How are you?"

"Never been better. How's the number two lady in my life?"

"Anxious. Can't wait to get this over with so we can move on."

"You okay babe? I'm sensing something is wrong."

"No. Just a case of déjà vu." I told him.

"Please don't worry. Nothing is going to ruin this day. Not even BJ coming back from the dead," he tried a humorous approach.

"I wish you didn't refer to her by your old lover's handle."

"Sorry. I didn't mean anything by it."

"I know. It just makes me feel a bit uncomfortable."

"Duly noted."

There were a few minutes of dead silence between us.

"Babe?" he finally said.

"Yes?"

"I love you."

"I love you more," I said. "I'm going to call the number one lady in your life and I'll see you when you get here."

"Leaving in a few."

We exchanged sentiments and disconnected the call. I dialed Charlie's number.

"Mommy! Mommy!" I could hear Violet yelling in the background. I'm sure she knew it was me, even though she couldn't read. Charlie had programmed the word, Mommy, into his caller ID. She knew what that word looked like.

"What are you doing to my baby?" I teased him.

"My angel is going to be the death of me."

"Uh-oh, what'd she do this time?"

"Well, Uncle Charlie was shaving and that little devil ran off with my shaving cream, screaming, *Bubbles*. There's cream everywhere!" I couldn't help but laugh. That was my little mischievous one.

"Glad you find that funny. I'm sure it wouldn't be as funny if shaving cream was all over your house."

"That's why you have a maid and I don't. "

"Touché' my love, touché. Here's your little devil."

"Mommy!" Violet exclaimed when she got on the phone.

"Hey pumpkin. Is Mommy's little angel giving Uncle Charlie a hard time?"

"No Ma'am. No bubbles," she tried to explain that the foam wouldn't' make bubbles. I decided to wait to reveal that I had bubbles for her and that I would give them to Uncle

Charlie at the wedding. Realizing she wasn't coming down from her high anytime soon, I asked to speak back to Charlie.

"You gave her sugar didn't you?"

"Just a mini blueberry muffin."

"Glad she's with *you*." I laughed. I had told Charlie numerous times that even an ounce of sugar would have Violet bouncing off the walls.

"Love you much!" Charlie told me.

"Love you too Chuck. See you later." With that, I hit the end key on my cell phone and focused on myself. I said a long prayer, took a deep breath and stepped into my wedding dress.

I sat in my chair for a moment, daydreaming about becoming Mrs. Stuart Humphries. It was a long time coming and nothing was going to stop us. There was nothing that could ruin this day for us. This was it. This was my fairytale ending—the man of my dreams, the best little girl a mother could ask for and a lifelong friend. I was blessed and I knew it.

I could hear people moving about upstairs. My bridesmaids had come downstairs to offer last minute assistance. I studied myself in the mirror. I loved my new look. I just hoped Stuart would like it.

"I guess it's that time," I told Angie. "And where's my baby?"

"I'll go up and get her and let everyone know that we need to get this show on the road."

I was puzzled when Angie came back without Violet. She had a disturbed look on her face.

"What's wrong?" I asked her.

"I don't know. No one has seen Stuart *or* Charlie."

"What?" I exclaimed. Here I was already stressed out, and these two were somewhere lollygagging around . . . not to mention the fact I wanted to see my little girl.

I asked Angie to hand me my cell phone and dialed Stuart's cell number. After a few rings, it went to voicemail. I tried a few more times with the same results. I tried the hotel he was staying at and the desk clerk told me Stuart had checked out already.

I tried our home number . . . voicemail. I dialed Charlie's cell phone and got the same results.

I tried Charlie's home number . . . voice mail. I was becoming frustrated and worried. Butterflies played tag in the pit of my stomach. It was unlike Stuart *or* Charlie not to answer their cell phones when I called. I calmed down and asked Angie to go check again. Again, she came back empty handed.

I must have had a look of horror in my eyes because the bridesmaids started whispering amongst themselves as Angie moved into my personal space and coddled me like a colicky baby.

I made every attempt to save what little make-up I had on but my tears had a mind of their own.

"Why is this happening?" I asked no one in particular. "Are you friggin' kidding me?"

Again, I dialed Stuart cell number. A few rings . . . voice mail. Then I dialed Charlie's.

"Hello?" the voice on the other end answered. I was thrown for a loop because the person that answered was not Charlie. I must have dialed the wrong number, but then again, I did enter the number I had programmed for his assigned speed dial number.

"Um, uh. Err . . . I must have dialed the wrong number."

"No! Wait. This is Officer Henderson. Who am I speaking to?" he asked. I started to hang up but decided not to.

"My name is Renee Matthews. I was trying to reach my friend."

"What's your friends name ma'am?"

"Charlie . . . Charles. Charles Thatcher."

"Ma'am, there's a problem and I 'm going to need you to come to my location."

"Why? What's going on? Where's Charlie? Is he in trouble?"

"Ma'am calm . . . "

"Where is he? Where is my baby?"

"Ma'am . . . ?"

"Where is my little girl?" I was sobbing uncontrollably at this point. In between sobs, the officer managed to get in a few words. The only thing I heard was . . . *accident . . . come quick . . . no time . . .*

Angie grabbed the phone from me. "Hello, this is Angie. I'm Renee's friend and today is her wedding day. If this is your idea of some sick . . . "

"Ma'am. Unfortunately, this is not a joke. There's been and accident and I need you to bring Ms. Matthews to the I-8/I-5 connector. We're right at the end of the I-5 southbound off-ramp.

"We'll be right there," I heard Angie say. Within minutes, we had borrowed a car and we were on University Avenue headed towards the highway.

I kept asking Angie what happened, but she would only say, "Renee, calm down."

How in the hell did she expect me to calm down? I couldn't find my child, my soon to be husband and my best friend. No one would tell me anything.

As we drove down the highway, I could see police cars, fire trucks and paramedics. Part of the highway was blocked off.

"You have to find a detour. We need to get to my baby."

Angie didn't respond. I had no idea how she planned on getting past the accident. She passed the off ramp and headed towards the roadblock.

"What are you doing? You're wasting time. I need to get to my baby!"

Angie brought the Mercedes to a stop. She turned to me and grabbed both my arms.

"Renee, listen to me. I need you to calm down."

"Stop telling me to calm down. I need to get to my baby!" I continued my rant and Angie remained silent as she stared at me.

After I came down from my lunatical tirade, Angie looked towards the accident . . . I looked too. For the first time, I noticed that in the midst of the medical personnel, fire trucks and police, was the tangled metal wreckage of Stuart's Range Rover and Charlie's town car.

I gasped for air. It couldn't be. I reached for the handle but Angie tried to stop me.

"Renee, wait!"

"That's Stuart's truck and that's Charlie's car!"

A police officer walked in our direction and motioned for me to roll down the window.

"Are you Ms. Matthews?"

"Yes," I said, trying to calm down. The last thing I needed was to be arrested for going off on San Diego's finest.

The police officer opened my door, took my hand and led me towards the wreckage. Angie got out of her car and followed us. The closer we got, the weaker I became.

Angie was the first to see Violet's bloody body pinned under the town car. She tried to shield my sight, but in doing so, she inadvertently turned me into the direction of Stuart's truck and that's when I saw him. I screamed uncontrollably. I tried to run towards him but two offers intercepted me. My heart dropped as my world came crashing down around me. I screamed.

"Nooooooo! Noooooooooooo!" I sobbed uncontrollably. Somewhere in my turmoil, I could hear one of the officers tell Angie that I probably shouldn't be there, but there was no way I was about to leave.

"Violet! I need to get to my baby. She needs my help!" I struggled and loosened myself from the officer's grip and ran towards the town car, but stopped within a few feet and fell to my knees. Violet's body was partially pinned under the mangled mess as Charlie's lifeless body held onto her torso. I tried to get up and get to my baby. I had to get her from under the car. I had to get her to the hospital to get her cleaned up and make sure she was okay, but each step I tried to take seems like running through quicksand.

I tried to scream for the paramedics to help me get my daughter to the hospital, but nothing came out of my mouth. My lips were moving but no one could hear me. I finally managed to bring myself to my feet. I took two steps closer to my angel.

"I'm coming Angel!" I mouthed. A few more steps and I would be able to get her from under the car, hold her and get her to a hospital. "I'm coming Pumpkin. Mommy's almost there." I took another step . . . and then . . .

I blacked out.

Epilogue

It had been weeks since I had lost everything that had ever meant anything to me. I thought God was cruel taking them all at once. I was still mourning Violet, Stuart and Charlie. I asked him repeatedly why it had to be me. I knew the scripture *The Lord giveth and the Lord taketh away*, but I didn't understand how it was relevant to me and my life. It was so unfair.

I could smell myself. I hadn't taken a shower in days and still had on my pajamas. I hadn't eaten in days either, with the exception of a box of crackers and a bottle of water. I picked up the eight by ten portrait that I had clung onto since the funeral. Stuart, Charlie and I had taken Violet to Sea World and we took a photograph with one of the dolphins.

I remembered that day as if it was yesterday because Violet was so excited. She sat on her Uncle Charlie's shoulders as a dolphin leaped up to give her a kiss. She was so ecstatic. Everything that ever meant anything to me was featured in this photograph.

I questioned God for weeks. I know this was his doing. The fact that Charlie and Violet's car crashed into Stuart's as they were all on the way to our wedding, proved to be more than just a coincidence to me. Only God could be so vivid, yet so unclear in his message. When Barbara Jean had died, I felt a sense of clarity and closure, but now, I felt so lost, broken and alone.

I had taken a leave from work and refused any visitors. My phones rang off the hook, until I decided to disconnect them all from the wall. I had heard several knocks at the door, and the doorbell rang repeatedly. I had ignored it all. I didn't want to be bothered by *anyone*. I wanted to wallow in my pity. I had made repeated bargains with God that if he brought my daughter back, he could take me instead. Unfortunately, my rational self knew that God didn't make those types of deals.

On this day, I was finally getting back to reality. I still couldn't believe that my family had been wiped out in one instance, but I was starting to realize that I had to get myself together. I knew that eventually, if I didn't start answering the phone or the door, someone *would* knock the door down.

I got up to go to the bathroom and nearly vomited at the smell in the room. After I accessed the foul odors, I realized that it consisted of my body odor, stinky sheets and spoiled food coming from the fridge. I stripped the sheets from the bed. They had been on the bed since the last night Stuart and I had slept there. My vision became cloudy as I cried and violently removed the sheets from the bed and threw them onto the floor. I fell into the heap crying controllably.

I tried once more to get myself together and dragged my frame to the shower. I turned on all six heads and let the nearly scalding water hit me where it may. I soaked my sponge with body wash and tried to scrub myself into non-existence. Once again, I collapsed to the shower floor, crying uncontrollably. I stayed there for a while—until the water turned lukewarm.

I finally gathered enough strength to get out of the shower, dry myself off and put on a clean change of clothes. I looked at my hair. It was a hot mess. Luckily, Shena had cut it short. I was able to brush it back.

As I brushed my hair back, I looked at myself closely in the large mirror. I looked as if I had aged at least ten years. The circles under my eyes were dark and my eyes were blood red. I lost all lack of judgment when I saw Stuart appear behind me as he whispered, *Get yourself together and move on with your life. It's what I want for you. I want you to be happy. I will always love you. It's okay. Open your heart.*

I was startled but was relieved that the last few weeks had only been a dream. I turned around to embrace Stuart, but he wasn't there. I turned to look into the mirror once more and only my wretched shell stared back at me. I knew I was starting to lose it.

I took the sheets that I had stripped from our bed and took them to the laundry room to wash. On the way back, I stopped by Violet's room. It was in the same condition she had left it before she went to spend the weekend with her Uncle Charlie. She was such a princess—a girly girl. Her pink sheer canopy floated above her bed as the sparkles from it, bounced light from the bright sunlight onto her pink walls.

That little girl was very meticulous when it came to her room. I found it odd for a two-year-old child. Everything was in its place, with the exception of Lara Jones Campbell's *Goodnight Poppy Cat*. I remembered that day like it was yesterday. Violet had forgotten to put the book away because she had an epiphany as she ran into our room and jumped on the bed.

"I would like a kitty and a puppy!" she shrieked.

"Oh you would?" Stuart laughed.

"Yes sir!" she nodded with precision.

"And who's going take care of these animals?" I asked her rubbing the top of her head.

"Aunt Sonja," she responded. I laughed. If Sonja knew that in addition to being Charlie's housekeeper and assistant that she'd have to take care of two pets, she might not be so happy about it.

"We'll see, okay?" Stuart said. Violet looked at him as if she was studying him. It seemed as if she had done this since the day she was born. She was daddy's little girl and she knew just how to work him. If daddy didn't comply, she'd work Uncle Charlie. Those puppy dog eyes pulled at Stuart until he finally gave in.

"Okay, okay. We'll go look for a pet next week. But *only* one at a time. So, you'll have to decide if you want a cat or a dog first." He nudged her nose. She ran off in glee. I knew what was next. She was off to call her Uncle Charlie to seal the deal.

Violet was no fool, in fact, she was the smartest two year old I knew. She did it every time. She'd talk her father into something and then she'd call her Uncle Charlie to ensure that if Stuart didn't do what he said, Uncle Charlie definitely would. Her plan was to get her father to buy her a cat, and her uncle to buy her the dog.

After Violet left our bedroom, I shook my head at Stuart. "You sucker."

"What?" he asked cluelessly.

"That baby works you every time, and then sucks Charlie in to make sure you follow through. The sad part is that neither of you realize it."

I was shaken out of my thoughts when I saw a form out of the corner of my eye. I looked to my left and saw Violet sitting on her bed, in the pretty flower girl dress that I had packed for her to wear at the wedding.

Mommy, it's okay. We are here waiting for you. You have to play the game first so you can be with us. You still have things to do before you can come be with us. Daddy and Uncle Charlie said hello and they love you. Finish your work so you can come be with us. Love you Mommy.

The image of my little girl dissipated as I found myself on the floor, again, trying to cry away the pain. Why did God have to take my little angel? What work was she talking about? What things?

I never made it downstairs to resolve the stench in the kitchen. I fell asleep on the floor next to Violet's bed.

I was awakened the next day by the annoying sound of my doorbell. I was still in the same spot—on the floor at the foot of Violet's bed. I looked up at the digital princess clock on Violet's wall. It read 10:11 a.m. I sat there for a moment staring at the clock as if I could will it off the wall. Whoever was at the door was not going away. Suddenly, the ringing stopped. It was about time whoever it was had gotten the message.

Much to my disappointment, whoever was at my door had given up on the doorbell, but I soon realized they wanted in. I crouched down and crawled to my bedroom when I saw the door handle jiggle. I checked the security panel on the wall, just inside the door. The system was secured. I went back into the hallway and positioned myself at the edge of the catwalk, overlooking below.

Whoever it was had a key. Right before the door opened, the security alarm was disarmed. I panicked and ran into the laundry room. The door was open now.

"Señora Renee! Señora Renee! Are you here? I was worried about you. Are you here?" It was Sonja. She had used Charlie's key to get in. I was sure she was one of the many people who had been trying to reach me.

"Sonja you scared the hell out of me!" I said as I came down the stairs for the first time in days.

"I've been calling you and when you didn't answer I had to come . . . "She stopped in mid sentence. "What is that God awful smell?" I nodded towards the kitchen. She walked toward the smell, mumbling in Spanish. "!Caumba, apesta acqui dentro!"

"No shit Sherlock," I said, hot on her trail. Surely she didn't think she was the only one who could smell it. I plugged my nose as I opened the fridge. The odor magnified and nearly threw me back.

"I need you to shower and I'll take care of this," Sonja said, pushing me towards the staircase. I sniffed my under arms. What was she trying to get at? I didn't stink.

I headed upstairs to shower. I prayed to God to give me the strength to at least be somewhat functional. I had several things to take care of—things like Stuart and Charlie's financial affairs. I wanted to open a non-profit organization in Violet's name. I had to search for a new house and put the current one on the market. I knew if I intended on retaining an inkling of sanity, I could not stay here.

I dressed and joined Sonja downstairs. Much to my surprise, she had completely cleaned the kitchen and was working in one of the bathrooms.

"My, you work fast Querido," I told her. She gave me a beautiful smile. "Do you like this house?" I asked her.

"Si."

"How about I give it to you." She looked at me with joy in her eyes, but then it quickly turned to disappointment.

"Give? Do you mean you'll live elsewhere?"

"Yes."

"Ah. I don't know if I can do that Señora. Señor Charlie made me promise to look after you."

I looked at her perplexed. She explained.

"Señor Charlie made me promise that if anything happened to him, or Señor Stuart, that I'd watch out for you."

"He told you that?" I asked.

"Si."

"When?"

"Before Violet was born. He was updating his will and he made me promise," she said.

I walked into the kitchen and sat on one of the stools at the bar. That Charlie always made sure that I was taken care of.

"Did I say something to upset you?" Sonja startled me when she walked up behind me.

"No Sonja. I just remembered how much I miss him . . . all of them."

"*Ah*, it's okay. You will get through this," she hugged my shoulders. "I miss them too."

She told me that she would finish the cleaning once she returned from the market.

"If there is anything in particular that you'd like, please write it down on this piece of paper. While I'm gone, I need you to weed through your voice mail." I smiled. I may have felt alone, but I wasn't alone. Charlie had made certain of that.

After Sonja left for the store, I went into my office to reclaim my life. I checked my home voice mail first. There were several messages from Sonja, my secretary, Susan, Stuart and Charlie's attorneys, an insurance agent, a few co-workers and people from church.

I wrote down the important messages down and erased the rest. Next, I checked my office line and retrieved messages from Sonja, Pearl, my secretary, co-workers and clients. I took note of those messages and called my office.

"My word!" Pearl shrieked. "Darlin', we've all been so worried sick about you. How are you?"

"I'm hanging in there. Ready to get my life back on track and try to regain a sense of normalcy."

"I totally understand. I am here for you, whatever you may need."

"Thank you Pearl. Please thank everyone for all the cards and flowers. I really appreciate it." She gave me an update on my client's statuses, new policies and procedures of the office and new products and services. We were on the phone for at least a couple of hours.

When I was done, I was famished. I smiled to myself—another one of Charlie's words. When I stepped into the hall outside my office, I could smell something good coming from the kitchen. Sonja had returned and the house was spotless.

I found her in the great room going through mail. "What is that delicious smell? It almost smells like *Menudo*."

"Si, it is," Sonja said. "I knew it was one of your favorite dishes. Mi madre taught me how to make it."

I hurried to the kitchen, towards the lovely, spicy aroma. I used a ladle to spoon the delicious Mexican soup into a wooden bowl. Sonja had toasted fresh tortillas and sliced avocado to go with the dish. "Sonja, would you like me to bring you a bowl?" I asked.

"Please Señora," she responded. She hadn't taken her eyes off the mail she was looking at. She had a serious look on her face. I fixed her a bowl of soup and brought it to her on a serving tray.

"What is it?" I asked her.

"I think you need to read this," she said handing me the multiple sheets of paper. It was a police report—the police report from the accident. The letter that accompanied the report stated that the investigation into the accident had been concluded. My heart began to sink as I read the police report.

Jonathan Fallon, was the driver of vehicle number one. Jonathan was Charlie's driver. I continued to read the report. *Passenger number one was Violet Justice Humphries and Passenger number two was Charles Thatcher. The driver of vehicle number two was Stuart Humphries.* I read over the rest of the police report and stopped when I got to the crash description and crash events.

It has been concluded that vehicle number two crashed into vehicle number one as it entered the highway from the off-ramp. It is estimated by the evidence at the accident scene that vehicle number two was going in excess of ninety-five miles per hour. It has also been concluded that the driver of vehicle number two was in the process of sending a text message upon impact with vehicle number one. The driver and passengers of vehicle number one were killed upon impact, as was the driver of vehicle number two.

I couldn't read any more. I began wailing and screaming. Sonja held me as I fell to her feet. This was all my fault. I had killed my family. I had sent Stuart a text and he was answering my text. I caused my husband to be, to take his eyes off the road. I killed my family. I killed my little girl.

Jesus why?

Sonja knew I didn't expect an answer. She just held me and wiped my face. We remained in that position for at least a half hour.

"I need to be by myself," I told her and ran upstairs to Violet's room. I laid in her bed and hugged one of her stuffed animals.

"I'm so sorry. I didn't mean it," I repeated. Again, I wondered why God hadn't taken me instead of my family. I was crying so hard that my eyes were swollen, and I could barely see through the slits. That was probably why I could barely make out the human form that had appeared in front of Violet's bookshelf.

"I told you I wanted to be alone Sonja!" I snapped.

"Babe. This is not your fault. This is all a part of God's plan." It was Stuart. I sat up in the bed. Two more forms appeared.

"Mommy, we love you. Hurry up, Mommy," Violet said.

"Luv, everything happens for a reason. God has his reasons. We are still with you. Take heed in the message that is being presented to you," Charlie said.

"What message? I killed the only people I ever loved—the only people that ever loved me. How could I be so selfish?"

"Renee, the love we all shared was . . . *is* priceless. No one can ever take that away. We experienced a love that others will never have the privilege of experiencing. We were blessed. You *are* blessed. Bask in what we shared, not what you've lost. We will all meet again. When *He* thinks you are ready, you'll join us, but until then, reflect on the positive." I wanted to reach out to Stuart, but I was afraid if I did, I'd realize that they weren't real.

"We love you," all three said in unison. With that, they disappeared as fast as they had appeared.

I thought about all the good times. I smiled. I prayed. I thanked God for what he had given me—what he had allowed me to experience. He had taken a poor wretch like me from the chains of my past and placed love and happiness in my life, even though only for a little while. I smiled, and cried and did it all over again.

I finally gathered my composure and decided I wanted to watch home movies. I knew that would cheer me up and help me shake myself from my funk. At that very moment I knew, I'd never have any more children, I'd never love a man like I loved Stuart and I'd never have a friend as great as Charlie. I was okay with that . . . for now.

When I got downstairs, Sonja was still going through mail and other paperwork.

"What's that?" I asked her.

"Señor Charlie's will." I could see a tear escape her eye as she handed it to me. I hadn't given a second thought to

Charlie or Stuart's will. I reheated our soup and I sat the tray down on the coffee table and sat a bowl in front of each of us.

"Can I see that?" I asked.

"Si. This is your copy."

Sonja handed me the multi-page document and I began to read it. My eyes got bigger than I thought possible. I looked from the paper to Sonja and then back to the paper. I knew Charlie was rich, but I had no idea. According to his will, he had left twenty million dollars to Sonja, along with his home in San Francisco and his condo in Mission Valley. He left her a part of his investment portfolio and other assets. It didn't surprise me. Sonja had been a faithful employee and friend to Charlie for years.

I continued to read on. To Violet, he had left a fifty million dollar trust fund and to me, he left . . . I couldn't breathe. I held my chest. I looked at Sonja again.

"It's an official document. The attorney has been trying to call you. Charlie left this copy in his safe," she explained.

"But *two-hundred million dollars?* This has to be some type of mistake." I didn't even read the rest of the allotment, although if I knew Charlie well, he left tons of money to various charities.

"No Señora, there's no mistake. Señor Charlie loved you very much." I sat in a daze for moment. How I would have rather had Charlie than any amount of money. This could not, would not, replace him.

I went to the kitchen and pulled back a makeshift cabinet that hid the safe that Stuart and I had installed. I retrieved its contents and returned to the great room.

Both Stuart and I had drawn up our wills and took out life insurance on each other, *and* on Violet. I started studying the documents. The payout on Violet's insurance policy was fifty-thousand dollars, while the payout on Stuart's life insurance was two-million. I scanned his will and noticed that it had been updated.

He never told me he updated his will.

The documents specified that I was the beneficiary of five-million dollars, and other investments and a custodial account in Violet's name in the amount of two-million dollars. I had to admit, our lifestyle allotted us anything we wanted, *whenever* we wanted, but as I sat and looked at the figures. I was a bit taken back.

✝   ✝   ✝

Sonja and I had run errands all day including visits to attorneys' offices and the bank. Now we sat in the great room of the house that Stuart, Violet and I had once shared. We looked at each other with exhaust.

"I'm sure going to miss Señor Charlie and Señor Stuart and especially Lucerito Violet."

"Lucerito?" I asked.

"Little bright star," Sonja explained. I smiled.

"I am going to miss them as well. It will take some time to heal, but I know that they'd want me . . . they'd want both of us to live on and never forget them."

Sonja and I shared a long embrace. "I have a suggestion," she said breaking our embrace.

"And what's that?"

"Before we make any decisions, let's take a long vacation," she suggested.

"Where would you like to go?"

"I would love to visit me famalia in Mehico and then maybe Hawaii and even New York."

I laughed at her. "Wow, from one extreme to the other eh?"

"What about you Señora?"

"Sonja, please call me Renee. We are sisters in spirit."

"Renee," she smiled. I returned the smile.

"I would like to visit Atlanta. And of course, all the other places you mentioned. Perhaps Jamaica or the Bahamas. Hell, we can go anywhere we want."

"Tell you what, let's start in Mexico, work our way to Hawaii, the Islands and end with New York and then Atlanta. How does that sound?"

"Sounds good to me!" she said. We were excited, yet exhausted. We leaned back on the sofa and channel surfed before we both fell asleep.

Later, we called our travel agent and set up our exploratory vacation. We'd leave in two weeks, which would give me time to get some work done and tie up a few lose ends. I had no immediate intentions of quitting my job. It was one of those things that drove and challenged me. I had plenty of time to decide what my next steps would be. I was thankful to God and to Charlie for giving me Sonja. I don't think I could have made it without her.

After I got myself together, I swore I was going to concentrate on finding her a man. As for me, I had loved and lost the two men that I loved the most in this world. There would never be anyone who could fill that void. I had been gifted more love in the short time I had with Stuart, Violet and Charlie than most could ask in an entire lifetime.

They would forever be in my heart and with me. I was content . . . for *now*.

There is a time for everything, and a season for every activity under heaven:
~~Ecclesiastes 3:1 (New International Version)

Also by Yolanda M. Johnson

YOLANDA M. JOHNSON-BRYANT is the author of Circumstances and other novels. She is currently working on her children's, teen and tween series, her That Literary Lady Knows series, her Tommy Lane Detective Series and a host of other projects. When Yolanda isn't writing or spending time with her family, she enjoys being a career Toastmaster with Toastmasters International and a mentor and volunteer for Junior Achievement and the Women's Resource Center of Greensboro. She is a technology and social media geek and loves giving workshops on literacy, self-publishing and social media. She is the owner of Bryant Consulting and Literary Wonders Media Group. To find Yolanda on the web, just "google" her. Her websites are: www.yolandamjohnson.com, www.thatliterarylady.com, www.literarywonders.com and www.bryantconsultingonline.com She and her husband, Greg, reside in the Piedmont Triad area of North Carolina.

www.ingramcontent.com/pod-product-compliance
Lightning Source LLC
Chambersburg PA
CBHW071713140626

46557CB00011B/80